TALES FOR DREAMERS

VOLUME I

ANITHA KRISHNAN

DREAM PEDLAR BOOKS

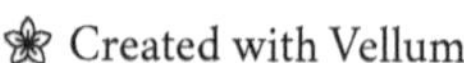 Created with Vellum

For anyone who has ever dared to dream,
Your dream exists because you do.

~

For Dhruv & Abhinav,
This is our dream life, the one we're living.
How lucky I am! How tremendously lucky we are!
Thank you.

~

ABOUT THIS BOOK

TALES FOR DREAMERS — VOLUME I

Welcome to The Dream Pedlar's emporium of delightful dreams and wondrous whimsies, of impossible illusions and fleeting fantasies!

Behold a captivating collection of 100 flash fiction tales where the mundane morphs into the magical, the everyday shape-shifts into the exceptional, and the inconceivable becomes the inevitable.

Where witches promise to reveal the secret of happiness and wise old men whisper wisdom and warnings in your ears.

Where you summon an angel and the devil appears instead. Where billboards flash messages from the afterlife and Gods mess with the desires of your heart.

Where woodland creatures host tea parties and pirates are on a recruitment spree. Where trees lead a secret rebellion and reindeer go on strike.

Where the months of the year debate over how many days each of them truly deserves.

Perfect for lovers of fantasy and whimsy, for seekers of the paranormal and the uncanny, this collection of fantasy fiction stories invites you to a hundred different sojourns in wee worlds of whimsy and wonder. Even the briefest of wanderings into these tiny tales of speculative fiction will leave the most lasting of impressions, the kind that lingers for a lifetime.

Because the magic you seek has also been yearning to reveal itself to you.

BEFORE WE BEGIN

Dear Reader,

This book has been more than a decade in the making.

In every creative's life there comes a moment when they realize what exactly it is that they wish to create and manifest in the world.

I was pulled to the call of writing in my early twenties, at the turn of the millennium, as it came to be. But it wasn't until after an entire decade of meandering, trying my hand at different kinds of writing, that I stumbled upon the kind of stories I really wanted to tell.

My heart skipped many beats when I read Tanuja Desai Hidier's *Born Confused*.

My soul galloped with unbridled joy when I read Erin Morgenstern's *The Night Circus* and later stumbled upon her *flax-golden tales*, little nuggets of fantasy paired with an image.

Then came Diane Setterfield with *The Thirteenth Tale* and *Bellman & Black* and threw open the doors to sheer magic and boundless possibility. I've just finished reading Setterfield's *Once Upon a River*, and it reminded me of all the reasons I fell in love with writing fiction in the first place.

There was so much to love in all the beautiful prose and imagery these authors wove that I managed to pen *Hello, Dreamer!*, the introductory soliloquy to this collection, solely to express how exactly I wished for my writings to enchant readers.

It was also my first post under the online moniker, *The Dream Pedlar*, which I use to date.

Incidentally, I published this post on my birthday many moons ago. On Saturday, 20 November 2011.

See the mathematical harmony in that date? 20/11/2011. Even the stars were aligned in my favour that day!

That day marked the beginning of my journey into the kind of writing that has really shaped me throughout the years. Whimsical. Speculative. Touching. Heart-breaking. Soul-shattering. Yet, comforting too.

Still, it took a few months after that first post for me to begin writing these tales in earnest. I labeled them *'tricks from my hat'* at first.

My first run lasted six months; I posted a new tale every Sunday and Wednesday. Then I slowed down to posting once a week. Somewhere along the way, I stopped altogether. Only to resume a few years later when I moved from Singapore to Canada. Again, for just a few months.

This on-off cycle took place several times. The labels underwent many variations, changing almost each time I resumed writing and publishing these stories after a hiatus, whether brief or far too long.

I don't remember when and how the label *'tales for*

dreamers' took hold. But it seems apt. Just perfect for these little tales of whimsy and wonder.

Ever since I started publishing my books, I've wanted to publish this collection of tales. The biggest hurdle was in figuring out how to include the images that inspired these tales. That task was so daunting for so many reasons that I kept putting off the project.

Earlier this year, I decided to resume writing and posting more *Tales for Dreamers* on my website. I've always loved writing these tales. Now I post them every Friday morning at 9 AM EST.

Coming back to writing them from a place of greater maturity and wisdom than my younger self had possessed more than a decade ago, with a better grasp on that omnipresent fear of whether or not these stories will be read and loved by an audience, is turning out to be an entirely different and much more wholesome experience altogether.

That's when I took stock and figured out that I had inadvertently written more than 150 such tales to date. The desire to publish them in book format, in different volumes, year after year, sprung up again.

I wondered: What if I were to publish these tales without their accompanying images? Would they hold on their own?

Turns out they can. They very well can.

As I've been reading and re-reading these old tales while putting them together for you, I can't even seem to remember the original image that inspired them. New visuals have been cropping up in my head. Delightfully, so.

This gives me the confidence that you too will enjoy reading these tales on their own without a predetermined image to distract you from the impressions and imprints the words themselves will leave on your mind.

The stories are whimsical enough. Powerful enough. Fleeting enough to cast a lasting enchantment on all who turn the page.

~ Anitha Krishnan
Burlington, Ontario
Thursday, 30 January 2025

HELLO, DREAMER!

Mesdames, Messieurs, poppets and imps, mischief-makers and trouble-seekers, I have for you, for all of you, for each and every one of you, dreams of all sensations and durations.

Dreams that will take your breath away, fantasies that will thrill and overwhelm, illusions that will leave you spellbound. Reveries for the noontime, or nightmares for the witching hour should you have a penchant for the shivers.

Illusions that last a few moments, or flights of fancies that never end. Age-old dreams that were dreamt into existence by the Gods themselves. Some others as pristine as a newborn, and some rare ones yet undreamt of.

Come hither, my dearies, for your dream-rides. No two dreams are alike. But to choose one, you must let go of the rest.

Ah, choices! You have countless dreams to pick from, but only one can truly be yours today.

To the beautiful lady in green; may I recommend, Madame, the Story Tellers and Yarn Spinners. They appear in your dreams and tell you a different story every night. Their tales are mostly pleasant but sometimes terrible too, I must warn you.

But you know how it goes with dreams. We barely let them run their course and so they come to haunt us, day and night, and again the next day and night.

The Story Tellers and Yarn Spinners will tell their tales every night, and I hope some day you will find within yourself the courage to follow your dream until the very end.

Dear Sir in the grey bowler hat, pray tell me what ails you. Is it the several decades of existence that wear you down? Or the memories of youth and damsels that make you nostalgic? Ah, so it is adventure you seek, Monsieur.

Voila! What you need is this rare, glossy shell of the brave tiger cowrie whose thirst for adventure remains unquenched. It is said the tiger cowrie set out to master the art of metamorphosis so he could swim in the depths of the oceans, gallop through the vast muddy terrains of man's land and soar across the vast expanse of the skies. L'océan, le terrain, et le ciel, traversing all in his single-minded pursuit of adventure.

Slip the tiny shell under your pillow and ride along with the tiger cowrie every night mon ami, but remember, adventure comes readily to the seeker only after he casts away his shell.

A-ha my little poppet! I have just the perfect dream for you. The Quick Fingers, it is called.

Magic tricks that have been passed down from generation to generation, their secrets preserved only in the hands and minds of the world's greatest illusionists. All the sleights of hand that have ever been performed, illusions that have left countless spellbound and dazzled.

You will be the sole audience of the Quick Fingers every night, my pretty child. They will teach you conjuring tricks and illusions and chicaneries and other feats. For years, you will learn by night and practise by day.

And eventually, when you learn to merge the magic from your dreams with your waking life, may you find yourself on a stage much larger and glamorous than this, the world lying at your feet, bedazzled by your skills.

But remember ma chérie, each maneuver can be performed only once. Any attempts at recreating the same magic will undoubtedly be futile.

Now, let's see. You, my dear.

Yes, you. You who are here yet not with me.

Would you like a dream too? A dream, perhaps, of riches and fame? Or a fantasy of everlasting happiness?

But I doubt these would do you any good. The other ones didn't anyway. The ones you have tucked away into the dark folds of the night. And there they remain hidden all day. Come morning and you barely recall your dreams of the night. So little use you have for them and they for you.

What you need, my dear, is a tale. A story with a moral. A tall tale, perhaps. Or maybe a short one. It doesn't matter. As long as it is a tale.

Once upon a time, long long ago, in a far, far away land ...

Oh, you've heard this one, haven't you?

Very well, let's see now. How about the one in which a little girl falls through a rabbit hole and meets a mad hatter and the Queen of Hearts ... So you know this one too.

What? The story of the Dream Pedlar? A tale about me? Well, how could I possibly... Are you absolutely certain? Is that what you would like to hear? Er... What could I possibly tell you about myself?

Perhaps I could talk to you of my past but oh, that would be so futile. I am no longer what I once was. Each dream changes me slightly but irreversibly. I now go by so many names that none can claim to wholly stand for me.

I am all your dreams and thoughts and desires and fears and impulses and yearnings interlaced into colourful braids. I am all of it at the same time but also not just any one of it. You could pull a loose thread and try to unravel me but I would only fall apart and crumble into so many fragments you would never ever be able to put them all together.

Sometimes I am the happy summer afternoon you drape over your shoulders like a warm quilt. At times, I am also the raging wind and the furious thunderstorm that screech and howl behind you and make you run for cover.

Perhaps I am the ginger-haired lass who bows her violin to soulful tunes on the street corner. Maybe I am the next-door neighbour you never see. Or the old homeless man breathing his last on a broken bench in a forgotten park. Or a sweet smelling bud beginning to bloom.

I am what you seek. I am also what you are running away from. Often I am both. More often, I am neither.

I could very well be your white-winged guardian angel. But then, I could just as well be that sinister looking thing creeping up from the darkness behind you.

1

THE ORACLE

The frog emerged only three times a year. On the first day of the New Year. On a day lying on the fringes of autumn and winter (his favourite seasons). And on a day that was chosen by vote.

But as the number of people flocking to see him grew year after year, the town council decided to request for more frequent or longer appearances. The frog, on the contrary, decided to keep his visits secret.

The mystery of his appearances was, at first, alluring to the townspeople. They spent several days lined up outside the pond, hoping to catch the first glimpse of him if and when he did decide to appear.

Soon summer rolled into autumn, and the children were the first to tire of the wait. They became cranky and their mothers took them home. Their fathers followed soon after as they needed to chop firewood for their homes before winter fell. Only the old and the crippled and the homeless and the dying remained.

That year, it snowed for the first time in the little town. A few kind-hearted people, bless their souls, brought food and blankets for the townsfolk huddled beside the pond.

As the days grew shorter and the nights harsher, someone said it was a good idea to build a temporary shelter with a direct, unobstructed view of the pond. And so it came up, a home run by volunteers for the brave ones lying in wait, with a fireplace and plenty of food and warmth and love.

The frog emerged on the first day of the New Year. At sunset.

Most of the townspeople were still wandering in a daze, recovering from the previous night's celebrations, their New Year resolutions already half forgotten.

Only the old and the crippled and the homeless and the dying remained still waiting in the shelter beside the pond.

"He's here," someone screamed, and they all shuffled and limped and hobbled out as fast as they could to behold the frog.

The frog beamed at them for a long time.

When he finally spoke, he simply said, "Good things come to those who wait."

2

———

CHOICES

The bottles came in a set of three. At first, I did not quite take to the one with the spray pump although I was besotted with its amethystine hue.

But the salesgirl refused to sell the pieces individually; it would bring bad luck, she was adamant. She insisted I try on each one, perhaps that would change my mind.

My fingers first headed towards the russet-coloured one. I lifted the stopper and dabbed some perfume on the inside of my left wrist.

At once I was enveloped in an odour of tea and earth and mint, spices wafting from my mother's kitchen, baby shampoo and the delicate smell of my baby sister's locks, Caramel panting in our backyard after a mad morning spent chasing his tail, a wintry nip in the air, the comfort of freshly laundered clothes, cotton candy and popsicles, the wonder of possibility.

I next turned to the dainty one in purple and squeezed the spray pump. Soft white fumes as if from an incense stick drifted forth and snaked over me, in and out of my hair, garlanded my neck, twirled around my ankles and calves and over my heart and around my wrists and up my arms, and I was blinded as if by a thick fog that had rolled in from the sea.

In my mind's eye I found butterfly colours on my fingertips, fairy rain, a piece of blue sky here, a tuft of white cloud there, the cool touch of a silvery anklet on my skin, a lover's heartbeat, happiness, sorrow, then happiness again, freedom, life, loss, a new lease of life, a new life, the smell of roses, poetry, longing, the ease of letting go. It was everything my present life was made of.

By now it was evident the third bottle held my future.

I caressed the translucent green container in my hands and with more curiosity than trepidation I withdrew the stopper.

I peered inside.

It was empty.

My disappointment must have shown on my face.

The salesgirl quickly covered my hands in hers and said, "You are lucky. You have the gift of choosing your future. Not all of us have that choice."

~

3

A WHOLE NEW WORLD

I never did trust the Pied Piper. His reputation preceded him, but not everyone wanted to see him for who he really was.

He was a charmer, perhaps a descendant of the cunning folk. So when he arrived in town touting his promises of a whole new world and new beginnings and how everything would be transformed in the blink of an eye — "like magic," he promised — most of the townspeople fell for it.

It did not take long for the townsfolk to split themselves into two groups, those in favour of and those opposed to the Piper's promises.

"Out with the old, make way for the new," the Piper's supporters chanted.

"Don't get carried away, you fools!" cried the cynics. "The grass is always greener on the other side."

"Frogs in the well, that's what you will all remain," mocked the champions of the Piper's cause.

"Better than the shallow roots you lay everywhere," their opponents quipped.

And so on and so forth the two groups quarrelled. The aficionados sought to induct more townspeople into their clan. Whether by persuasion or coercion was irrelevant. What mattered was an increasing number of supporters of their cause. Change or be changed, was their motto.

Lovers were torn apart, families were in shreds, friends turned their backs on each other owing to differences of opinion. Old relationships were ruined, and in their place newer ones were forged and linked tenuously by communal interest.

The day the Piper played his pipe, his followers sang in merry voices. Yours was the loudest and the happiest. His music and your song led the way.

By the light of the setting sun, the ardent crowd of devotees coursed through the town in a trance, leaving broken hearts and deserted houses in their trail. A whole new world and new beginnings awaited everyone on the other side of midnight, the Piper promised.

It was quite poignant, you know, the way you all danced through the town. Drums beating, hearts thumping, feet tapping, voices chanting. Like a carnival that was about to swoop up and drag all the joy and life and magic out of the town in its bacchanalian departure.

The euphoria was infectious. Our resistance weakened. Some of us joined you out of curiosity, some to partake in the festivities. But mostly none of us wanted to be left behind to clean up the lonely confetti of memories the next morning.

You waved out to me, whether in beckoning or farewell, I could not tell.

I shrugged my shoulders and said to myself, "So what if we can't see eye to eye, you and I can still be together."

And I joined the cavalcade.
So now there's you and me.
But also everyone else in between.
Only the lame one tottered behind me.

4

A PRICE TO PAY

Everybody had to pay a price to pass through the tunnel. Those who didn't, never found the light at the end of it, the tunnel spirits made sure.

But it wasn't dosh that exchanged hands. No. These were the times when people and all other beings took you at your word. A promise made was a promise kept.

The crux of the matter was that you had to part with something you held very close to your heart.

So when the little boy stood at the entrance to the tunnel, his heart tugging at him to skip down the green passage, he promised to give up candies and pastries for a week. When he emerged on the other side, beaming and glowing as if he had been kissed by a fairy, he said that the tunnel had appeared to him as a log of Swiss roll, green endlessly twirling in green.

When it was her turn, the young maiden clutched at her heart and promised to yield to the tunnel spirits the memories of a long lost love. On the other side of the passage, she found herself once again ready to love and to be loved.

The young soldier gifted his longsword to the tunnel spirits and exited a free man, liberated from the battle scars on his heart.

Everyone had a price to pay. Some surrendered the hurt of forgotten friendships. Some others paid with their vices, and in some cases, their virtues. The cynic pledged to stop finding fault with others. The coward agreed to part with his fear.

By the time I found myself at the mouth of the tunnel, I had made up my mind to hand over my soul. It was truly the thing closest to my heart, the only thing I had.

But the tunnel spirits said they could not accept it. They did not take lives, they said.

"Could you please take my soul only for safekeeping?" I asked. "Take it and hide it somewhere deep within you where nothing and no one can find it," I pleaded. "And then some day we'll have fun looking for it in all the wrong places," I threw in for good measure.

The tunnel spirits named their price in response.

They asked me to stop seeking permission to be happy.

5

THE CHRISTMAS TREE

I don't exactly remember when the Christmas tree started to shrink but I suspect it was around the time both my Dad and I stopped believing in Santa Claus.

It was the year Dad stopped decking out in Santa's garb for his nocturnal shenanigans to make our Christmas presents appear mysteriously under the tree.

It was also the last time I had stayed up all night waiting for a white-bearded plump old stranger to come sliding down the chimney, if that were even physically possible for him, with his stash of gifts for all of us.

No one knew why the tree had started to shrink.

Dad theorized that it was all relative; I was growing taller and so the tree appeared to be growing smaller, he declared. What I didn't have the heart to tell him was that I was growing up too quickly and that his explanations were no longer quixotic enough for me.

I turned to Mom who said the tree must feel weighed down by the frosted glass baubles of oversized wishes and hope that hung from its branches year after year. It's a pity, she said, we can't even drape tinsels and fairy lights around the little thing anymore.

Gran said we would now have to be careful what we wished for. It couldn't be too large as it would no longer fit under the tree. It need not be too small but you'd have to make room for others' wishes too, she said. I asked her what she wanted this year and she said that a fistful of happiness and good health was more than she could hope for.

Last year the tree was barely taller than our parlour palm houseplant. That year the boyfriend had sewn for me a soft toy, a little pup that held its heart in its mouth with the words *puppy love* stitched on it. This year I could do with an engagement ring, I thought.

6

GHOSTS

*Y*ou know they exist.

Soft footfalls on the stairs.

A shuffling in the shadows.

A scurrying in the attic.

A knock on the door by an unseen hand.

An unfriendly gust of wind that sweeps up your hair and chills your blood on a still summer night.

The sweet smell of roses that ripples past you, and evanesces in a breath.

Silvery streaks of light that whiz past the corner of your eye. There now, gone the next instant.

Little, floating orbs of light you see with eyes shut.

Fragrant fumes from an incense stick, twirling and vanishing in mid-air.

An empty glass of wine you are sure you washed and dried last night, now found lying in the sink laced with sanguine dregs.

The rocking chair, never still.

Love stains on the carpet. There now, gone tomorrow.

Things you lose, things you find. A family heirloom that wriggles out of your fingers in your sleep, turns up on the kitchen countertop months later when you stop looking for it.

Memory playing tricks with your mind. The little pranks they play on you.

Doppelgangers, the cleverest of them all. Gifted impressionists. You look in the mirror, you can't believe what you see.

A strand of grey hair, and another, yet another. Crow's feet. Wrinkles around your mouth. You just can't believe what you see.

The brown eyes, your own, only older. They wink back at you. A figment of your imagination, you tell yourself.

The voices in your head. Louder and clearer than any you have ever heard. You think you are losing your mind.

They rise from the cracks in time. Like the second hand that falters ahead, a heartbeat too slow. The grandfather clock, whose pendulum swings a tad too fast.

They thrive on the fringes of reality. Like at the end of a dream. When you are about to fall into eternal sleep, they pull you back to safety.

It's a tightrope walk. One step in the future, one in the past. Imagination ceaselessly morphing into memory. Belonging to neither this world nor the other.

They are not the bad sort, not really. They mostly like you. Amused by how you can see but not believe.

Sometimes they take offence when you believe in things you cannot see — like God — but refuse to acknowledge their existence.

The little clues they leave for you. The tinkle of wind-chimes, a rosebush that refuses to grow, a forgotten photograph in monochrome that falls in your lap, the letter that never arrives, the stranger who does you an unexpected good turn, the black cat that disappears into the night.

They don't like to be ignored. But you pack up and leave, make your way to someplace less spooky.

They are left behind, like jilted lovers. They roam the corridors, flit in and out of walls in their frantic search for you, for life.

The house crumbles under the weight of their grief. Colours are washed away by their torment. Gardens wither. Sunshine is now a stranger in these parts. Grey and forbidding, haunted houses speak of joy that was once there, now long gone.

But you know the ghosts still exist.

～

TO THE MOON AND BACK

When the amusement park project was abandoned for want of funds, the street urchins made it their joint, explains the stripling as he leads us through the grounds. He looks no more than fifteen or sixteen.

At first, they did nothing other than lying on the grass and smoking a reefer, convinced this was all there was to life, that they had seen it all, and that little else mattered.

Until one of them suggested they take a go at the ferris wheel one misty evening, he says as a faraway look creeps into his eyes.

He recounts how with what sounded like a melange of a groan and a wail, the big wheel had started to turn and taken him and his friends on a trip more lucid than any they had been on.

As the big wheel turned, so had time. Moments had turned on their head and distended to eternity. Happiness had stretched over the boys' faces like snug-fitting masks. Their breaths had hung in the misty air, forming steaming rings of white life around the revolving wheel. Time and space had mingled in unbridled harmony in their juvenile minds. The world was at peace at last, they had believed.

He then leads us to the carousel, a hum playing on his lips. Another misty evening they had mounted their noble steeds on the merry-go-round, he recalls. An invisible hand had started to play the music and, as if on cue, the animals had leapt into the air. Dragons and unicorns had galloped through the mist, flying their riders into the twilight.

They had raced with moonlight and shooting stars, soared past birds flying back to their nests, screamed in thrill when their steeds nosedived to kiss the ocean, and lain with carefree joy on their backs as night draped their world in a blanket of stars.

The roller-coaster is the trickiest of them all, he warns, and says it had taken them a long time to figure out how it works.

Only one passenger is permitted to ride at a time. You mount the train and whisper your destination to the wind, and only then does the train start with a rumble, he explains. He has never ridden it before, he is not ready yet, he says, but he thinks he knows what lies in store.

At first, he says, the train creeps harmlessly uphill, inching ahead until you are able to kiss the clouds, and as you pause to take in the view from above, the train quietly slips from under you and gravity yanks you earthwards a split second later, and if you are very lucky you fall back into your seat right before the train arches backward into a vertical loop, then attempts another somersault and yet another, and just as you begin to think you could get used to the momentum the tracks disappear and the train freezes to a halt in the nick of time, and flings you out of your seat towards outer space, with a snort as if it were spitting phlegm from the back of its throat.

And where would we land, we ask.

On the moon, the lad says. Or among the stars if you miss it.

And how would we get back, we demand to know.

You don't need to, he shrugs. When you're ready to leave, there is no coming back.

$\sim$

ALL IN A YEAR'S WORK

All months were born equal. The circle of the earth around the sun was divided into twelfths and each month received an equal slice.

Until December stirred up a commotion one day when he declared he felt outdone by January because everyone spends most of December looking forward to the New Year.

Poppycock, retorted January. This was utter nonsense, she remarked, and said that in fact people love December because he has Christmas and most of the year-end holidays all to himself — "He sits on the best days of the year like a fat broody hen," were the exact words she used — and that when she finally arrives on the scene, the celebrations have all but come to an end.

"And since we are on the topic," January continued, "I ought to remark that it is I who must feel threatened." Not that she did, she hastened to add, but if any month could be permitted to feel woeful about his or her lot, it was her, she claimed. Everyone begins the year on a high note and it takes them only a single month, which regrettably is January, to fall back to reality with a thud, she said and banged her delicate fist on the table for effect.

"Show me one person who has spoken a true word on the last night of December," she challenged, as if it were all his fault that she started with a bang and ended with a whimper.

She turned an oblong face towards February and pointed a slender manicured finger at him, demanding he put his pennyworth in.

Now February was a lovely child and he preferred to steer clear of any conflicts that erupted among his clan. But he was especially fond of December, who resembled a pot-bellied pipe-smoking Santa himself, and equally intimidated by January who was still glaring at him through her lorgnette.

February cleared his throat and said, "I don't quite see the point of your dispute. As for myself, I am perfectly content with the present state of affairs. With Cupid playing tricks, everyone seems to have a jolly good time."

"Spoken so truly like someone in love, foolish and irrational," dismissed January coolly.

"I think that's true for me too," piped up March. "Not the foolish bit but the happiness part of it. I put the spring in everyone's step," he said. Think of it, he went on, the world passes through an equipoise in March. "I tame the endless nights of winter to make way for the vernal freshness of April," he puffed his chest.

"To be fair, March," interrupted September, "That is not a specialty unique to you. That is precisely what I do when it is my turn in the bottom half of the world."

"That hardly merits any argument," huffed December. "It is not merely you September, we all lead dual lives. Shall we stick to our conventional roles for the sake of this discussion? When you think of Christmas, what comes to mind first — snow or beach weather?"

September acquiesced in silence. December gestured to April who then spoke up gently. "To be honest, I am often confused about my place in the scheme of things," she said. "Am I spring or am I summer? Or am I to adapt myself to the whims and caprices of each year as it comes?"

A profound silence enveloped the room. December looked benevolently at dainty little April, her eyes blue as freshly laundered skies. Even January's face softened a little but she caught herself lest the others should misconstrue her expression as a change of heart. "Are you unhappy with the situation, April?" she asked.

"Oh no no, January," April laughed. "It was just a thought. And with March and May by my side, I am never lost. I turn to them whenever in doubt. And looking on the brighter side," she continued, "I begin on a hilariously tricksy note, don't I? Anyway, don't you worry about me. I was merely taking stock of my life. Like all of us are doing."

January remained quiet.

December cleared his throat.

Time halted for an indecipherable moment.

A wisp of doubt began to form in April's mind. "That is what we are doing, aren't we? Weighing up our lot in life?" she queried.

"Uh, yes-yes," December said and with a hasty wave of his hand passed the oratorial baton to May.

May dragged on her cigarette deeply and with a bored look on her face said, "You can call me spring, you can call me summer, you can call me whateva you like baby. All Aa know is this. Ma job is to let the su-uhn shine. You know what I'm sayin'?"

She drew on the white stick again, the mentholated flavour forming clouds of ice in her mouth which she puffed away in thick rings. "Some like it hot, some ain't gonna like it hot," she resumed. "So Aa let the sunny boy do as he pleases. If he's gat bones to pick with someone, Aa say to him - Give it to 'em baby. You know what I'm sayin'?"

"Aa ain't got no identity crisis and all like little April here," she patted April on the head. "But Aa am touched by your loyalty, little sistah. Anytime you gat a problem, you come to me. Don't you go running nowhere else. You know what I'm sayin'?"

January barged in on May's monologue. "Yes, yes May, we know what you're sayin'," she said in mock imitation. May winked at April and retreated into the recesses of her mind, wearing a nonchalant look on her face and breathing out puffs of silvery smoke.

All attention turned to June. "There is a reason I have the longest days in the year," June said crisply. She took turns to look everyone in the eye as she spoke. "It is so that we have time to do more, accomplish more. Not sit around a table talking absolute, inconsequential drivel," she snapped and glared straight into January's eyes.

July intervened almost immediately. "Dear folks, please allow me to apologize," he began. "You must forgive my twin sister. She has had too much on her mind lately, what with people moping about in the realization that half the year has flown by, perhaps the best half of the year," he said and immediately won a gracious smile from April and even January allowed herself a little blush that flamed her cheeks. August and September snorted, December narrowed his blue eyes under thick, bushy eyebrows, which July ignored. The majority were swept up in his flamboyant charm. "As for myself," he continued in a pretence of humility, "I am merely here to remind people not all is lost with the end of June. Come to July, is what I say."

"Every court needs its jester," December muttered to himself, then raised his tone before any eyebrows shot up. "Very well July. Now August, surely you will have more fascinating things to say. Some more fascinating things, I mean," he added with a twinkle in his eyes.

"If you are referring to the multitude of personas I hide within myself, December, you will most certainly not be disappointed," August said genially, and his smile crinkled his eyes. "There's the sunshine and holidays in some parts of the world. Then there are the wet days in other parts. Having to wear many hats all at once, never knowing which one will come in use now. Unpredictable, like life itself."

December clapped heartily. "It is obvious why you are called August," he gushed. "Lofty in thought, regal in bearing," he effused.

A stony silence followed.

"He got the hots for him or what?" someone whispered, deliberately audibly.

"Ssshhh!" January hissed. "Let's move on," she commanded.

September cleared his throat and said, "I stand on the fringes of summer and autumn. I have long days and short ones. Summer is bidding farewell, making room for a brief autumn before winter takes over. I reside on the threshold, in both places at the same time but also in neither entirely. I think it is important for me to remain where I am, in the midst of transition, embracing the change, and helping everyone through it."

December clapped, and everyone joined in the applause

this time. "Well put, September," he cheered. "Bravo," someone shouted and another whistled and yet another hooted.

When the applause faded, everyone turned to October. But his chair was empty.

"Where's October?" January asked.

When nobody responded, she repeated her question louder this time. "Where the hell is he?"

"You know the little devil," July laughed. "He may have very well gone out for a quickie," he guffawed.

"Shut up, July," snapped June. "November, you might as well give your performance and then we could call it a day. I have plenty of matters needing my urgent attention," she said.

An expletive was beginning to form on January's lips when she spotted a dark, shapeless figure rise from behind September. The shadowy form billowed out and spread like a thick cloud of blue-black smoke over everyone's heads. There was a distinct chill in the air, a harsh sting caught the months unawares.

From the screen of smoke emanated images of streets ablaze in scarlet glory, trees in autumnal blossom, their colours reflected in the skies, bloodied by the setting sun. The ball of fire sank into the ocean and the room was plunged into opaque darkness.

From the night leapt a figure onto the table with a thud; a pink-faced clown dressed in suspenders so large it could have hidden a twin under its garments. A red bulbous nose protruded from its face, which was plastered with a smile so wide it reeked of evil. It held out a black magician's hat and shouted, "Trick or treat!"

January shrieked, February clapped, March stomped his

foot in disgust, April swooned, May blew a ring of smoke towards the clown then splashed water on April's face, June pursed her lips and hissed "Codswallop", July remained frozen in his seat, jaw hitting the floor, all his charm now a stranger to himself, August let a knowing smile play on his lips, September shook his head in exasperation, October was still missing from his seat, November raised a middle finger towards the clown, and December chuckled at the expressions on everyone's faces.

"You trickster," December cried, choking on his laughter as tears streamed down his cheeks.

October bowed deeply, pleased with his performance. He reset the atmosphere and his clothes with a snap of his fingers and returned to his place beside November.

Words were conspicuous by their absence on the lips of everyone but August and December, who congratulated October on his fine act.

It was an incensed November that rose from her seat to talk about her life. "Trust October to steal the show," she bawled. "Sandwiched between two childish attention-seekers, I obviously am left with very little for myself, be it time or space or attention. What has the world come to? There's talk of Halloween well after I have begun. Christmas trees spring up in November these days. New Year plans are made in November. It is as if I do not exist at all."

She sniffed, then paused for a long moment, drew in a deep breath and, as if she had had some kind of epiphany after a long, trying day, shook her head and said, "I am sorry. I'd rather not ruin the valedictory."

November pulled a case from her purse, flipped it open, powdered her nose, coloured her lips, shut the case close, and tucked it away. "Let's begin again, shall we? And

October, you better sit still this time," she kicked his shin. "I do not have much to say but the thing I love most about being November is all the babies that are born in this month. Conceived by lovers under Cupid's spell in February, the little ones come into the world in November. It does not matter that winter is lurking in the shadows, the days are growing shorter and the nights endless, that December is getting grumpier" — she winked at him cheerfully — "or even that the year is almost coming to an end. A new beginning can happen anywhere, anytime," she said. When she sank back into her seat, she received a standing ovation.

And that is how it came to be that December and January each have their share of one and thirty days, because by the end of that evening, December had gotten to decide for himself and January had refused to settle for anything less than he had.

March was granted more life; everyone needs more time to adapt to change, he had argued. By the same measure, September was accorded another day which he politely declined; I am only executing my duty, he said.

May gained an extra day too, which she promised to share with April should her little sistah ever need it.

June, everyone concluded, was overworked and that it would be a shame to burden her more. But everyone could do with a little more charm, so July went one up on his sister on that count.

August scored points for his regality, and October for his bold performance. November said she already had more life than she could ask for.

February lost many of his days to others, which goes to show that if you are satisfied with your lot and do not ask for more, you may end up with less than before.

But all good deeds do not go unnoticed. To commemorate his sacrifices, February was rewarded with an extra day, but only once in four years. Being Cupid's friend, he remains everyone's favourite, which goes to show what matters in the end is not what you get, but what you give away fearlessly.

9

———

A GLIMPSE INTO THE FUTURE

*L*ater today you will set aside a moment to begin taking stock of your life.

All your pain, real and imagined. All your hopes, lost and never found. Relationships that strolled out the window and threw themselves over the edge. The troubling ones that lingered.

No, say not to me you do not have your fair share of loss, else you wouldn't be here now seeking a counsel and a cure.

This evening you will sever a relationship. Which one, I am unable to see, as you are yet to make up your mind. A walk in the moonlight will give you the courage you need tonight.

Tomorrow, as you sip your morning tea, swirling it in your mouth, feeling and tasting the brew like you have never done before, daybreak will begin to dispel the illusions of the night. What seemed courageous at night will appear foolhardy in the morning. And the first strand of doubt will begin to creep into your mind.

This weekend, you will go over the same ground several

times. Did you or did you not do the right thing? The questions never changing even when phrased differently. The answers, always the same.

But time tends to quell doubts, so by next week you will have convinced yourself this was how things were meant to be, and that you had no other choice.

In a month's time you will have forgotten most things. About him. About yourself. Life will see to that.

Until someday you bump into each other again, perhaps on the sidewalk, or in a dream or a nightmare. Some scars run deep. And the memories will come flooding back. The crinkles around his eyes, the melody of his voice, his laughter, the way you twirled your fingers in his hair, how his breath mingled with yours to create a flurry of lovers' air.

And you will come back full circle, setting aside a moment to take stock of your life again.

And the next time you seek a counsel and a cure, you will pick a better date to approach me. And I will foretell happier endings.

~

10

THE MISSING HEART

The King woke up one morning to find his heart had gone missing.

It had sprung from his chest at night, noiselessly in the din of his snores, snuck down his bed and across the thickly carpeted floor like a thief, jumped out the window throwing caution to the wind, and scuttered into the woods as if running for dear life.

That was the version of events the king shared with the royal court that morning (leaving out the bit on snoring). Truth be told, he simply did not know when and how and to where his heart had fled. But he could not bring himself to admit his baffled ignorance to his subjects, and so it was a concocted little tale that he shared instead.

Mortified that his heart had skedaddled, he called upon his commander-in-chief to lead a fourth of the royal troops into the forest at once.

"Bring me back the traitor," he bellowed. "He can't have gone very far, the little imbecile."

Days went by without any word from his men. After what

seemed like aeons only a handful of soldiers returned empty-handed and addle-brained, muttering incoherently of terrible loss and unspeakable danger in the woods. "Off with their heads!" hollered the heartless king and sent them marching to the guillotine.

He then commanded a third of his remaining troops to comb through the kingdom.

"Leave no house unsearched, no corner unexamined," he thundered.

The soldiers rummaged through homes and shops, markets and fields, gardens and streets. Walls were broken down, roofs were torn apart, the earth was dug into, birds' nests were ripped apart, wine barrels were struck open, crops were pulled out by the roots.

When the heart made no appearance, what began as a hunt soon devolved into plunder and pillage. For fear of losing their heads, the king's men ransacked the city and made off with their loot to the neighbouring kingdom. Infuriated, the monarch sent half of his remaining troops in pursuit of the defectors.

The rest of the king's soldiers remained in position, awaiting his orders, when one of them, a young pursuivant, piped up, "Has it crossed anyone's mind at all that the king's castle ought to be searched too?"

His comrades quickly shushed him.

"Have you taken leave of your senses, young man?"

"But think about it. This is the only place left untouched in the entire kingdom."

"You may be right, my man. But what if you are caught? Do you want your head to roll off that guillotine like a pebble down the hill?"

"If the heart is not found, we will all meet that fate sooner or later," the pursuivant sighed. "What kind of a heart is it that does not want to live with its master?" he mused.

"Perhaps it was a good heart."

"Too good for His Majesty."

"Indeed!"

Before long, the soldiers had made up their minds to sneak into the palace and look for the heart every night. They searched room after room painstakingly, taking care to put everything back in its place lest any suspicions should be aroused. But their quest was in vain. A search of the queen's chamber too failed to yield the heart. "Pity, he had never really given her his heart," someone observed.

On the last night of the search, when His Majesty had joined his wife in her room, the pursuivant made his way to the king's chamber. Moonlight bathed the room in eerie silver. His heart thumped with misgiving and he could swear he was being watched by unseen eyes crouching in the shadows. He took a deep breath, and ploughed on, first checking under the bed, then in the drapes of the curtains, and in the motes of dust that floated in the moonlight.

Once more his search proved futile and he slumped out of the chamber, head hanging low, now mulling the possibility of handing over his heart to the king if only to save his compatriots from the guillotine. Lost in thoughts, he ran into a wall. He backed a little and turned left to look for a way out and found himself facing the king.

"Your Majesty!" shrieked the pursuivant, and jumped back in fright. So did the king.

The officer quickly bowed and let loose a profusion of apologies. The king responded with silence. The officer finally mustered enough courage to look up, and saw the king staring back, bent in a half bow.

Our little spy slowly straightened himself and stood hesitantly. His hand crept to his chest and patted his thumping heart, wondering what to do next.

The king stood up too, hand on chest, lost in thoughts.

Was this some kind of joke, the officer wondered, but the king remained where he was.

That is when the pursuivant noticed the king was dressed in a tabard in faded red emblazoned on the front with the royal coat of arms, not unlike his own outfit.

A thought took seed in his mind. He stepped forward. When he was close enough, he held out his hand, palm facing the king's. Their fingertips touched each other's through the wall of glass. The officer then smashed his fist through the glass and retrieved the king's heart from the mirror.

"Why here?" he asked.

"A vain man's heart finds refuge in his mirror, the only place he cannot bring himself to destroy," came the reply.

The following morning, the king was a changed man. Humble and noble, he set about restoring his kingdom, looking to his heart for counsel every now and then.

As for the pursuivant, he was never to be seen again. Some claimed that he had to give himself up to the mirror. Some others swore they saw him at the break of dawn slinking out of the kingdom, carrying two sackfuls of gold and a broken mirror.

11

THE STORY OF A HORSE

Jobs were hard to come by in those days, so the horse decided to earn his keep working as a living statue.

At first he stationed himself on the pavement but as people began to spend more time inside shopping arcades than outdoors, he moved indoors. The owner of the mall did not mind at first — as long as we rake in more business, he said — and earmarked a special nook where the horse could stand all day long.

The children took to him instantly. They gathered around him, wondering at first whether or not he was real. He would sometimes wink at a kid or two, surreptitiously swish his tail over another's hair, and just as they'd begin to get used to his inertia, he would raise his forelegs in the air and nicker gently, startling and delighting the kids all at once, then come back on all fours and resume a statued pose.

Then someone decided it would prove good entertainment for adults if they started to bet on the horse.

And so they did, placing their bets on when the living statue would move.

At first, the horse obliged. A swish of his tail when the clock struck thirteen, a toss of his mane at the darkest moment of the night, a neigh at the break of dawn, much to the delight of the punters.

But after most of the public had had an initial good run on their wagers, the owner of the mall instructed the horse to curb the goodwill gestures. And so the horse began to stand still for endless days and nights, moving only often enough to persuade people to wager more.

They laid odds, lost some money, laid another wager, won a little, put more money on, and lost a whole lot more. Occasionally someone won a million bucks and it made front-page news, kindling hopes, reviving dreams.

It was funny how the horse died. He was growing old, his legs and neck stiff and sore from the tedium of his job. He eventually found himself incapable of motion. So when the time came, he simply froze in place.

And there he has remained ever since, everyone still unsure whether or not he is alive. Children gaping at him, imagining a wink every now and then. Adults betting on him, swearing a whinny was in the making. Anytime now, anytime soon.

And that is how the house always won.

～

12

OUT OF ORDER

The zaniest ideas always hit me on Friday evenings, even before I have sipped my first glass of Chardonnay, she mused.

Sitting on the broad windowsill in their living room, from where she beheld a panoramic view of the ocean, she smoked a More Slims, expertly blowing rings that took on the shape of her puckered lips and floated away and out the window, growing larger and larger until the fumes could no longer hold on to each other and dissipated in midair, fourteen storeys above ground level.

For a long time, she sat in silence, mesmerized by the duel in the crepuscular skies, awash with myriad colours, a mélange of purple, orange and red that set the scene for a battlefield.

It had become a daily ritual. The sun hovered over the far end of the sea, preparing to retire for the night. On the opposite end, the moon rose, pale and timid in the presence of the setting sun.

There was a moment when the two seemed to be eyeing

each other carefully, waiting for the other to make the next move.

The sun, merely a shadow of his former raging self of the day, yet more than a match for the moon. Holding on, unwilling to descend lest the moon should take over.

The moon, flimsy and shivering, unsure if she ought to rise further. Crawling upwards stealthily, waiting for the sun to disappear.

For one fleeting moment, it almost seemed as if the sun would regain his rightful place in the sky. It was that moment of uncertainty that spelled his doom. He plunged into the bloody ocean, spilling the last of his rays all over the world, conceding defeat, having overstayed his welcome.

As the sun bowed out, the moon sailed higher into the sky from the other end, gracefully, shining more lustrously with every ascent. Having conquered the sun, she rightfully claimed his light as her own. And then she covered the ocean with a silvery sheen, laying the sun to rest in peace.

She exhaled in relief. Dear cosmos, if I had a choice, I would be the moon, she whispered. The waxing and the waning moon, the full moon and the new moon, the restless shape-shifting moon, the one that makes oceans roar and wolves howl, whose light clandestine lovers seek out in the night, the one that drives men stark raving mad, frightening and alluring all at once, the blue moon, the orange moon, circling the earth until eternity, sometimes too close but always out of reach.

She lit another cigarette.

Night descended on her part of the world. Twinkling stars burst into view, Venus standing resolutely bright in the western sky, guarding the grave of the defeated sun.

I could be Venus too, she thought. Venus, the evening

star. Venus, the Goddess of Love. Venus, the Roman Aphrodite.

Fantasies are delightful, she concluded. But in reality, she was perhaps more like the princess trapped in the witch's tower. Fourteen storeys above ground level. Confined in midair, in an enclosed apartment. Their lovers' nest. Their first home, where she waited every evening for him to come back to her. He should be home any minute now, she told herself.

Her mobile phone beeped. It was a text message from him.

Honey, just exited the MRT. Walking home now.

She leaned over the window and scanned the roads below. She squinted her eyes and saw him enter the gateway to their apartment building.

Baby, she called out loud and clear. He looked up, not because he heard her but because he knew she would be waiting for him by the window. She always did. He waved out to her. She waved back.

She had to decide quickly. The moon, Venus, the princess — which one would she be tonight?

The princess, she chose. The princess, whose knight in shining armour had arrived.

Ecstatic, she punched the numbers on her mobile phone and called him.

Darling, I'll let down my hair, so that you may climb the golden stair, she said.

He paused. *Why honey? Is the lift out of order?*

❦

13

THE BIG PICTURE

I have often wondered what the big picture is.

When the boyfriend broke up with me, he said I ought to take a step back and look at the big picture. That maybe this wasn't meant to be. That maybe destiny has other, better things in store for us, he said among other such vague assurances.

When I was passed over for a promotion at work , the manager promised it would be my turn next year but said that for now I ought to look at the big picture and keep working hard, or better still, harder.

When I asked my friend why she had to die at such a young age, she did not give me an unambiguous answer but instead said that in asking questions such as these, I kept missing the forest for the trees and that it will all make sense in retrospect.

And so I decided to set out in search of the big picture. Something that would help make sense of it all.

And I looked all over, rummaging through maps and

time, history and almanacs, mountain tops and ocean floors, birthdays and obituaries, yesteryears and hereafters.

I kept looking until I reached the end of my tether, my nerves frayed, my mind unhinged from the constant wandering from one place and time to another.

It was only when I mounted the swing on the top of the world that I found my answer.

The big picture.

The city lay sprawled below me, brickworks and glass facades jostling for space.

Clouds littered above, interlaced in a fluid clasp.

And me in between. There in mid-air, legs dangling, no ground beneath me, no roof over my head, I saw everything around me, as far as the eye could see.

The big picture.

Always lying in between the lines.

Not in the breakups nor in newfound loves. But in the heartaches and the soul-searching quests in between.

Not in this tale nor in the next. But in the musings in the interim.

Not to be found in yesterdays nor in tomorrows. But in the here and now.

Like being in a very beautiful dream. Neither asleep nor awake, but being the most alive.

～

14

THE TEA PARTY

"The tea party begins at four," the old man said.

It was only a quarter past three, so he suggested we lie in wait by the bushes at some distance.

"They like neither visitors nor onlookers," he grunted. We huddled behind the thicket in wonderment, determined to not irk the partygoers.

The old man squatted down beside us, scratched his scraggy beard in a moment of thought, then proceeded to narrate to us the history of the place.

"Folklore has it," he began, "that the first tea party took place even before mankind came into being but obviously there is no documented evidence of this. It was the wood creatures that established the tradition of the tea party. It began as a weekly affair.

"Back then, nectar was the beverage of choice. Wood creatures took turns at organizing the party — which meant sending out invitations, laying the table, ensuring everyone has a good time, breaking up fights caused between guests intoxicated by excessive consumption, and cleaning up the after-party mess before another fellow creature assumed the host's mantle for the following day. The guests brought along nectar and exquisite delicacies, along with news from their parts of the world. Births and deaths, sightings of new creatures, the discovery of new lands, new fruits grown and new beverages concocted, news from the mountains and the seas. The visitors gave each other the lowdown on happenings in their corners of the world."

The old man paused, then looked up at the sun and down at the shadows of the hedges, and nodded to himself. "Another half an hour, eh?" he said. We peeped above the hedges. All was still at the tea table.

"But the earliest credible record of the tea parties taking place as we know them today dates to the turn of time," the old man continued. "By then, the human race had existed and evolved for aeons, but it had taken man longer than it had the wood creatures to discover and share the wonders of tea and tea parties.

"At first the tradition had continued in its original spirit of social entertainment. The parties were mostly attended by residents of the neighbourhood. They were occasionally joined by travellers passing through the woods. The visitors regaled the guests with tales from faraway lands and adventures of their travels.

"It was only when the war broke out that the tea parties began to assume a more strategic significance. Soldiers and patriots and scholars assembled here to plot their defence strategies. The woods provided shelter to fugitives who brought news of the enemies' movements. Revolutionaries met in secret around the tea table where the seeds were sown for many mutinies and insurrections that were to take place around the world. There was never enough tea during the war, but the table became home to the ideas and plots and courage and bravery of the people that sat around it.

"But the enemy did eventually manage to penetrate the woods by which time most of its inhabitants had fled to different parts of the world. The ones who lived to tell the tale introduced tea parties in their new hometowns. The others who failed to escape were caught and beheaded by the enemy but the kind wood creatures rescued their souls. So they continue to live, only differently."

He wiped the sweat from his brow and a tear from his cheek. Another look at the sun and the shadows, and he gestured it was time.

An excited chatter began to ripple through our group but he put a finger to his lips and shushed. Like children up to no good, we covered our mouths with our palms, stifling giggles and murmurs of excitement, and peeped over the hedges.

Somewhere in the distance the church bells pealed. At the stroke of four, a merry chatter and hoots of laughter wafted through the woods. Cups and saucers rose and clinked in mid-air, an invisible hand tilted the teapot over the floating cups and filled them to the brim with tea. Scones and pastries, buns and cakes, and bowls of cream and jelly appeared on the table and floated on to plates as if by their own free will.

Unseen voices engaged in lively conversations. The guests talked about science and technology, mankind and civilization, endangered species and extinct ones, global warming and snowfall in summer, of hermits and spirituality.

One voice cooed with delight that humans were eavesdropping on their conversations, and some others reckoned it was alright and that we were only human and that it would do us a world of good if we followed their example and started to host tea parties such as this one.

15

IN WHICH YOU SEE THE
CONSEQUENCES OF MEDDLING
WITH THE TRUTH

The nations of the world were at war, spewing bombs and missiles at each other. Years of senseless killings had taught people to live in alternating states of fear and insouciance, and now they were getting accustomed to living without hope, which, if you really think about it, is a terribly tragic thing to happen.

Which meant that someone had to take matters in their hands, and the obvious choice for the job were the do-gooders, the meddlers, as the task on hand required them to stick their oars in everybody else's affairs.

An initial survey of soldiers and townspeople revealed that people felt most bereft of hope when they received bad news from loved ones; heartbreak and the ending of relationships were the most difficult to cope with, sometimes more difficult than news of death, the survey revealed. And so the meddlers decided they had to set right this lapse in communication.

So when letters were written and posted and sent on their way to different parts of the world, the meddlers secretly intercepted the messages, coaxed out the bitter words, replaced them with new ones filled with hope, and sent the notes on their way.

When pretty damsels sent Dear John letters to their men on the warfront, the meddlers saw to it that the soldiers were delivered messages of hope and love waiting for them at home when the war ends.

When the soldiers sent back home notes that spouted poetry and love, the meddlers erased all the soppiness. And the pretty damsels received friendly notes that unfettered them from their old ties — no hard feelings there — liberating them to pursue their newfound love interests.

The meddlers toiled away in secret, replacing profanities with apologies, hatred with compassion, bitterness with humour. And so the writers of the Dear John and Dear Jane letters began to believe it was a good thing to be truthful; after all they had received friendly notes of parting in response.

There were days when some of the meddlers wondered if they were indeed doing the right thing, causing people to live in illusory bubbles of happiness. Their chieftain allayed their doubts saying it was all for a good cause and that people in the town were now happier and no longer without hope.

"The damsels have moved on without guilt tying them down to the past," he said. "The soldiers are fighting their battles harder in the knowledge, albeit false, that their loved ones are awaiting their return. There is a bloody war going on and we need our soldiers to be strong and our people to have hope," he bellowed.

"But what will happen when the truth is revealed?" the doubting meddlers wondered.

"Truth has a way of making people get accustomed to it," the chieftain replied. "It is hope that we cannot live without."

It was all for a good cause alright because the war was won sooner than expected, the happy townspeople set about rebuilding their homes and neighbourhoods and their lives, and the soldiers returned home.

But when the Johns came back home to find their Janes in the arms of strangers, the truths came tumbling out like cats let out of bags.

At first there was shock and disbelief, anger and denial. But as the chieftain had predicted, truth prevailed and people have eventually learnt to live with it.

But now they are also getting accustomed to living without trust.

~

16

WHEN YOU MEET THE DOOR GODS, BE SURE TO LET THEM KNOW YOU'RE MY FRIEND. AND THEY WILL TREAT YOU WELL.

They stand guard on the threshold; they have stood there since the beginning of time, and for all we know they will remain at their posts long after we've traipsed in and out of several lifetimes.

Their role is to ask you questions each time you arrive on their doorstep, and your answers will help them decide which door they should let you through.

They usually get you to talk about your remaining dreams and desires, any regrets you may have and wish to express, any matters you'd like sorted before you step across to the other side.

They sometimes engage in a classic good cop, bad cop routine, but only if they have reason to believe you are not being entirely honest with yourself and with them.

So I suppose the best strategy is to come clean, lay yourself bare, because usually you find yourself on their doorstep when you have nothing more to lose.

Our turn came quite unexpectedly when we were out on a long drive by the seaside on a moonlit night; one instant we were on the road, the next we found ourselves on a path leading to the doors, as if transported by a wave of a magician's wand.

Several people queued up ahead of us, and each time we glanced back the queue appeared to get longer and longer.

It was difficult to say how much time had passed before we arrived on the doorstep; it could have been an instant or an aeon, all depended on how we looked at it.

Even before the Door Gods could speak, little Jeremy asked them excitedly if this was the entrance to the midnight fête we had been on our way to. They smiled at him in response, and said "Yes, if that is what you'd like." The door with the red-bearded guardian swung back and Jeremy hopped through.

When the boyfriend stepped up, they asked him if he wanted to go back to where he had come from. He thought for an instant, then (as I knew he would) replied in the negative, reasoning that one could never walk through life and time backwards. The door on the right swung back and he slipped through.

They asked me if I wanted to follow little Jeremy or the boyfriend. I said I wanted to follow my own path. I am not sure if that was the right answer but the Door Gods thought solemnly for a moment and both the doors swung back in unison.

I remember thinking in that instant that perhaps there were no right or wrong answers, only true ones. Because no one has ever walked through those doors and lived to tell the tale.

∾

17

OPEN, SESAME!

li read the signboard and scratched his head.

Surely he wasn't lost, was he?

He pored over the treasure map in his hands and mentally traced the path he had taken, comparing it with the trail scribbled on the map.

It was an old map, directions and crosses fading on paper now crumbling to the touch. The cliffs and valleys denoted in the map no longer existed, their places usurped by tall structures of blue glass and steep stairwells that led to underground cities.

Where Ali stood now was like a vast cave itself, several feet below the ground, made up of a criss-cross of different tunnels, each leading down unlit paths that disappeared around bends.

He looked down at the map, then up again at the glass façade. He was certain he was right outside the mouth of the cave that had once held an endless trove of treasure and where his brother Cassim had met his fate.

But the signboard confused him. It bore the instruction

in an elegant cursive hand: 'Try saying *'Open, Sesame!'* Or come to the main entrance.'

How could anyone be so foolish as to reveal the magic words so blatantly? Ali cursed.

Of course it was even more foolish to make no attempt at concealing the treasure within, he reckoned.

He reached out for the signboard, intending to take it down and burn it, but it was suspended behind the glass doors.

Open, Sesame, Ali whispered.

Nothing stirred.

Open, Sesame, he said louder.

Nothing again.

He walked around to the side of the glass-fronted cave, suspecting the 'main entrance' lay hidden here.

Another set of glass doors.

Another signboard there.

This one read, 'We are closed now. Opening hours 11 AM to 9 PM.'

Ali hadn't the foggiest idea what 11 AM meant but suspected it was a time of the day that clearly hadn't arrived yet.

Open, Sesame, he cried out again.

No luck.

In a fit of frustration, he kicked the glass door hard. It barely budged but promptly let out a prolonged howl that sounded to Ali like a wail of wrongdoing.

And before Ali could say abracadabra, three men sprang forth from the darkness, dressed uniformly in dark blue garments, wielding metallic contraptions that they pointed at him with a menacing purpose.

Freeze, one of them screamed.

Ali stumbled backwards and fell to the floor.

The three men towered over Ali, their weapons aimed at his chest.

One asked what business brought Ali to the underground passage at that time of the night.

He truthfully replied he was trying to get into the cave but that the magic words did not work anymore.

What cave?

Ali pointed out.

And why was he trying to get into the cave, another of the uniformed men asked.

To take home some treasure, Ali replied. *He and his wife had been down on their luck for a million nights now, and what with even genies demanding to be paid in gold for their services, he had had little choice but to return to the cave for more treasure. Only the cave had changed, as had the forest around it, and so have the magic words unfortunately,* he explained.

You have a genie, eh? the third man smirked.

Well, my friend, Aladdin, did. But now I do, Ali said but he could have immediately bitten his tongue off. From the bemused expressions on the men's faces, it was evident they didn't believe him.

And what are the magic words?

Open, Sesame, Ali said. The three men guffawed. *I would normally not have told you but it is written there for all to read,* he said.

Time to lock him up, the first man said. All three advanced towards Ali.

Perhaps you should ask your genie to come and rescue you, my boy, one of the coppers sniggered.

A feeling of dread overcame Ali. He quietly slipped his hand into his pocket and rubbed an old little lamp concealed there. He rubbed it thrice and screamed, *Take me home, Genie.*

A puff of cloud, a loud pop, and when the smoke cleared, Ali was gone.

An instant later, he and the Genie found themselves in their cave in the woods of Persia having travelled a million nights back in time.

This world is coming to an end, Genie, Ali said with a rueful grimace. *The new world will not have magic in it.*

And no genies to boot, Genie added.

18

A CRISIS OF IDENTITY

*I*t were moments like these that posed the greatest dilemma. What was he to do? Rise to the occasion? Or fall by the wayside? Was it the beginning or the end?

He lingered, looking for clues on the roseate horizon. Sunlight singed the clouds and they glowed like dying embers. A cool breeze fanned his part of the world. Unseen hands began to slowly drape the thick mantle of night on a part of the globe he had graced only moments ago.

The events of the past twenty-four hours flitted through the eye of his mind, one image segueing into the next. The morning rush, a full day of work with no respite, the sinking at twilight, then a red-eye to another part of the world before its inhabitants stirred. Each day no different than the other.

Often despair clouded his jaded mind. Surely there must be more to life than this, he wondered.

But then a sunny day lifted his spirits. Those were the

days he scaled the highest mountains, perched above the tallest cliffs, and beheld the world beneath him.

On days like these, he patted himself on the back for a job well done and readily accepted there was little more he could do here, that the people here were ready to light their own paths through the darkness of the night, and that it was time for him to spread his message in another part of the world.

Today was a day like that. A day spent usefully. Much had been accomplished.

Much more was to be done too but in another time and another place.

So when the moon started to rise from the other end, the sun decided to bow out gracefully. Not all battles need to be fought, he reckoned.

19

———

THE HOUSE THAT SPOKE TOO MUCH

*E*ven if mother couldn't always tell, the house somehow seemed to know whenever we played truant. Mouth open in disapproval, eyes staring at us in contempt, it was like a stern matron who ran a very tight ship. And the trouble was we couldn't talk to mother about it because that would have meant revealing the secrets of how we skived off school.

As we grew older, the house took it upon itself to express its opinions on the friends we brought home. Suffice it to say none of our friends received a warm welcome by the house; most were scared stiff by its severe bearing.

But it was only years later, when mother fell ill and we were compelled us to spend more time within the confines of the house to nurse her, that we began to pay attention to the goings-on within the four walls. Unexplained noises, the nocturnal rattlings of the roof and windows, stuff moving about in the din of the night.

And so when the queer little place was finally bequeathed to me, I jumped at the opportunity to put it up for sale and promptly moved to the city, hoping to find a girlfriend and start a new life.

They don't have houses here in the city. Too little space and too little time on people's hands to care for sprawling mansions.

Living spaces are all tiny enclosures of glass and steel, cozy little chunks of air neatly fitted one on top of another like indistinguishable building blocks. Unexplained noises in the attic are now replaced with the less distressing sounds of neighbours' quarrels and romps.

The house has not been sold yet. Not one interested buyer in the last five decades, which is hardly surprising. It has gone to rack and ruin now.

My children sometimes pester me to let them have a look at it but I am afraid what secrets the grubby old place would tell them about me.

20

A PARTY ON THE WAVES

My sister and I agreed that the house in the ocean, although abandoned by day, was used furtively at night. We asked Father and he said it was a place for fun *magicky* things. We wanted to pay a visit but he reckoned we could do so only if invited to.

We asked him if he could wangle an invitation for us but he sadly said he did not really know how one went about such matters but proposed that we whisper to the wind and hope the sea breeze carries our message to the owners of the place.

Seeing our crestfallen faces, he suggested we stake out the place for a night and see if we could find out more about it. And we jumped for joy.

Father helped us erect a little tent under the rocks by the beach. Mother filled a large picnic basket with sandwiches and cakes and ginger beer to last us all night. Caramel was tasked with standing guard over us all night, an undertaking he promptly accepted with a furious wag of his tail. My sister brought along Nutmeg, her stuffed unicorn toy, so he could keep vigil in her stead whenever she dozed off.

Father said it was quite alright if we began our stakeout after sunset; nothing really happens before then, he supposed. So we spent all day bathing in the sea and building sand-castles — with Caramel either yapping at our heels or chasing his tail or slumped in the sand, his tongue lolling out — casting an occasional glance towards the house, which remained innocuously still.

Evening came and brought with it sunset and twilight, in what order we couldn't be precise. When night fell, Father came to tuck us into our little makeshift beds inside the tent where we lay on our stomachs, propped on our elbows, staring at the house, which now resembled a shapeless mass only slightly darker than the black waters and the inky skies that enveloped it. Stars burst into the night sky but the house remained dark and opaque.

I don't know for how long we had been asleep but we woke to the wetness of Caramel's nose and tongue urgently rubbing against our faces. Bleary-eyed we looked towards the house. It was still mostly dark but soon tiny points of light began to drift in from nowhere and came to rest on the house.

We peered out of our tents and noticed that each time a light in the city was turned off for the night, a small glowing sphere made its way from there to the house in the ocean, which by now had come alive, fully lit with colourful fairy lights draped all over it.

Strange creatures rose from the ocean depths to the surface — my sister said she spotted mermaids and whooped with delight, I thought I saw selkies but I may well have imagined them, there was no way to be sure as all we could see were their silhouettes — and climbed into the house, which was soon drowned in tinny laughter and merry chinks of glasses and mesmerizing music that drifted towards our tent.

Caramel was torn between keeping guard over us and tearing down the beach to join the midnight party, but he resolutely held his ground beside us.

Nutmeg stirred from the back of the tent and quietly trotted out. He neighed and grew four times his size, and with a sweeping swish of his tail he leapt over the beach and splashed into the water, and in no time disappeared into the house.

When we woke up again we were in our beds at home and the sun was high in the sky. Caramel lay flopped at my foot, Nutmeg lay at my sister's bedside table, just as stuffed and dry and toy*ish* as he had been when Father had bought him at the store. Tied to his front paw was an invitation addressed to the four of us to attend a soirée on the waves tonight. I wonder what Father will say to that.

~

21

———

BOOTS FOR WALKING

The best thing about these sneakers is that they can take you to any part of the world you want to go to.

All you need to do is put them on, walk up the wall, and when you reach the top, simply jump and shout out a destination of your choice. And voila! That is where you will be before your feet hit the ground.

The tricky bit is not the walking-up-the-wall manoeuvre. That can be mastered with practice. The most difficult bit is getting your feet into the sneakers, or that is what we thought at first.

Because when One pulled them on, they seemed to fit his feet very well at first. But when he stood up and walked, the shoes began to shrink. A few steps and he gave the shoes a yank, screaming "Ow, ow, ow!"

When Two tried on the shoes, they grew larger and larger, and he said, "I bet I could fit both feet in one shoe," and he tried to but when he bent to lace it up, the shoelace wound itself around his wrists and kept them tightly bound until he kicked off the shoe, screaming "Ow, ow, ow!"

And we began to think the shoes were really mean and not worth trifling with. We made up our minds to return them to their previous owner, the old man at the edge of the woods, who had sold it to us in exchange for a nickel from One, a silver coin from Two, and a gold coin from Three.

But Three said he too wanted to try on the shoes, and so he did, and the shoes fit him perfectly like the glass slipper on Cinderella's foot. He laced them up, got up to his feet hesitantly, his feet snug in the shoes, which showed no sign of alteration. He gave them a moment, then smug in the knowledge they wouldn't trip him up, he ran towards the wall and with a hoop and a cry scrambled up the wall.

He was going to the city, he had made up his mind, the city of neon lights and mascaraed girls. But when he reached the top of the wall, he blindly stepped on a patch of slippery moss and lost his footing. "*Merde!*" he screamed, arms and legs flailing in mid-air, and landed predictably in a pile of dung.

We went to the edge of the woods to return the sneakers to the old man. When he heard our tale, it humoured him no end.

"The tricky bit is not putting them sneakers on," he cackled. "It is keeping your eyes on where you're headed."

22

LATERAL THINKING AND NONSENSICAL CHATTER CAN SOMETIMES LEAD TO A STORY WRITTEN BACKWARDS.

No one knew where the shark had come from. Nor why it had tried to gatecrash the party through the roof.

Someone suggested the shark may have jumped out of the water and landed a little too far out from the ocean for its own good.

Then someone else snorted and said sharks didn't do that kind of thing, only dolphins did the jumping-out-of-the-water trick, and then everyone looked towards the big fish sticking out of the roof and wondered what it was, a shark or a dolphin.

-It has to be a dolphin. Because if that thing did not jump out of the water how then did it land here on the rooftop?

-Maybe not, maybe it is a shark that was swooped up by a hungry dragon, which for some reason, I don't know what, somehow let go of the shark from its clasp and so now we have that thing sticking out from the roof.

-Do you reckon the dragon is also now thrashing around

on somebody's rooftop? I mean, something significant ought to have happened for him to have released his prey, such a huge prey that too, in mid-flight.

-If it were breathing fire down anybody's chimney, we would have heard about it by now. I suppose it is safe to assume that whatever made the dragon drop his prey did not kill or hurt him, perhaps just caught him unawares, shocked him a bit or scared him a great deal, so the dragon dropped the shark/dolphin/whatever-that-is but managed to recover enough, at least momentarily, so as not to fall down himself.

-Something that caught him unawares, shocked him a bit or scared him a great deal, eh? A sudden bolt of lightning? Mid-life crisis perhaps?

-It was a cloudless night, so we can rule out lightning. It could very well have been mid-life crisis. It did catch me unawares, and I did not even know what was happening when it happened to me, and it scared me a great deal. It still gives me the chills, thinking about it does. Yeah, the bugger must have had it real bad.

-I was in my forties when it hit me. How old do you suppose the dragon is?

-Oh, it has nothing to do with age anymore. Things are different in these times. It could grab you when you are in your twenties, thirties, forties, anytime. There is no telling when.

-Well, considering the size of his prey then, do you reckon he was trying to feed a flight of dragons? A family man?

-Are you suggesting there is more than one dragon?

-Why not? If there is one, there could be more.

-Then there would be dragon eggs too, isn't it?

-Yes, my memory these days is not what it once used to

be. But I recall reading in my childhood that dragons lay their eggs on mountaintops but take them to the mermaids for safekeeping in oyster beds.

-I remember reading this too. When the eggs are about to hatch, the mermaids bring them up to the surface. The eggs hatch in mid-air and the newborn must fly and breathe fire even before it can open his eyes to the world.

-And what if the baby is unable to?

-Tough luck. Have you ever heard of a wimpy dragon?

-That's it! This is a murder mystery and we are close to solving it too.

-Whatever on earth do you mean?

-What if this shark/dolphin thing had gotten greedy and had tried to sink its teeth into the dragon eggs? Papa dragon would have wanted to exact revenge, and voilà, he grabs the shark, drags him into the skies and lets go. Like he would have his newborn babies.

A hushed silence engulfed the neighbourhood. Everyone considered once again the marine creature, its tail sticking heavenwards, so out of place on a Sunday morning.

-How can you be so sure that dragons even exist in the first place?

-If a giant of a fish can be found wriggling its way into your home through your chimney, why can't dragons exist?

-There could be other explanations for that shark-dolphin thing on the roof.

-Yeah? Like what?

-Maybe it was being smuggled in an airlift and ... and ...

-And it fell through the floor of the plane?

-Yes, why not?

-Or there was a tsunami overnight that receded just as quickly as it had erupted but left no trace, nothing broken, nothing out of place, no missing persons, on the contrary a recent addition to the neighbourhood, that too a shark on the rooftop.

-Sounds just as plausible as your dragon theory.

-Yes, but it's definitely not as much fun.

23

SECRETS FROM THE UNDERGROUND

e never knew who they were but the creatures of the underground always gave us the answers we sought but only if we cared enough to ask and listen.

They did not always answer promptly; we had to follow a few strict rules and no exceptions were entertained.

First, you couldn't ask a question unless you had tried hard enough to answer it either yourself or with the aid of family and friends.

Second, you couldn't share the secrets you were told with anybody else. Cross your heart and hope to die.

Third, you dared not ask a question unless you were prepared to receive and face the truth for an answer.

Talking to them came in handy when as children we played hide-and-seek. Whenever I had a tough time as a seeker, I'd simply go put my ear against the trumpet that rose from the ground like a gigantic flower, and ask in my mind where the other children had concealed themselves. But only after a long, arduous search. And it almost always turned out that most of them had gone back home, having given up hopes of ever being found by me.

I once asked the creatures of the underground what I would be when I grew up. A princess or a magician? A queen or a witch? They said I would be a Keeper of Secrets and Mysteries, which at the time sounded delightful and exotic enough to keep me happy.

I run an apothecary these days but a few of my customers come every now and then to pour their deepest sorrows and darkest fears into little decanters that I then bury in the woods. And they leave a little happier, their souls unfettered from the secrets that had haunted them for so long.

I now ask the creatures more obtuse questions, the whys and wherefores of life. They still haven't answered me though.

I wonder if it is because I haven't tried hard enough to answer these myself.

Or am I not prepared to face the truth?

24

THE DEATH OF HAPPINESS

For all its promises of a jolly evening, the restaurant was cloaked in a funereal atmosphere the first time I entered it.

A large gathering of people — everybody in the restaurant barring one cowering in a dark corner — stood in a giant circle in silence, close to each other and holding hands, encircling something or someone I couldn't see but whose presence made itself felt in the warm glow of golden-white light that emanated from the centre of the circle and made all the beautiful faces shimmer with sadness.

When I reached near enough, two people unclasped their hands and quickly grabbed mine and let me squeeze through to be part of the ring.

In the centre lay a small, young fairy, writhing in agony. One of her wings had been severed and lay at her feet like a hand fan broken and discarded.

"What happened?" I whispered to the fellow on my right.

"Happiness is dying," the answer boomed from somewhere else in the eatery.

As if that were the cue they were waiting for, everyone started talking all at once.

"It was all Misery's fault."

"Happiness didn't stand a chance, she never did. She has always been so fragile, poor thing."

"Misery is savage."

"A bloody cat-fight it was, the two of them screaming and screeching and scratching and clawing at each other."

"That's what comes of being too kind to fight back. You only get killed."

"That bitch Misery, so selfish she can only think of herself."

"Why didn't you all try to stop the fight?" I asked.

An interval of silence.

A four-measure rest.

And the cacophony resumed.

"Here we fight our own battles, son."

"Yeah, you need to choose your battles carefully. Choose the ones you can win on your own."

"I don't agree with you," I countered. "You ought to have helped your friend. And it appears you haven't even tried to. So why are you all pretending to mourn for her?"

"That is not the question you should be asking. What you should demand to know is what punishment ought to be meted out to Misery now."

"Kill her, I say. Tear her limbs apart and set them on fire."

"Yeah, a nice funeral pyre it would make for Happiness."

"I thought you were merely mad. But now you are turning out to be savage," I said aloud.

"What then do you recommend, Little Sir? That we permit Misery to have good food and cold beer and dance around Happiness's corpse?"

"Well, you know what they say right? That Misery loves company? Why not just banish her from this place? She can spend the rest of her life moping about in solitude and trying to cling on to others willing to entertain her."

An interval of silence.

A four-measure rest.

"Not bad, eh laddie? I didn't think you had it in you but that is a brilliant suggestion, I say."

"A fitting punishment, one that will serve as a reminder of her crime for the rest of her life."

"Where's that bitch, hein?"

And in three mammoth strides, the tallest and the most towering of the men in the room was beside Misery, the little black bundle cowering and sniffling in the dark corner.

He grabbed her unceremoniously by her hair, swung her over his head in three swift circles, her screams getting louder and screechier with each turn, and flung her out of the window, and she flew in a wailing arc across the seven mountains and the seven seas. No one saw where she fell but we all felt assured it was far away enough for us to be concerned about.

The giant of a man dusted his hands with the satisfaction of a job well done. He turned to me and shook my hand and said, "Welcome aboard, son. Well deserved."

And with that, Happiness rose from where she was lying on the ground, attached her wing to her back and flew to the ceiling where she fixed herself for the rest of the night building a tapestry of night sky and stars glittering like disco lights.

The people in the restaurant came up to me, thumped my back and gave me hearty grins and cheerful laughters. Music swelled from nowhere and rocked the place rhythmically.

The bartender juggled bottles and glasses and concocted potions of ever-changing colours and flavours. Waiting staff scurried from table to table taking orders and with a snap of their hands they heaped piles of food quickly on the table tops. Someone put a chair under me, and a mug of beer and a plateful of food appeared in my hands.

When the food and drinks had finally suffused me with contentment, the mad people of the restaurant told me that they orchestrated The Death of Happiness whenever a newcomer made his way to the restaurant.

"Just a simple test you know, to make sure those who come in really choose to be happy, like the rest of us do, you understand?"

"I do. You are mad people after all."

Not long after a black cat slipped in through the window, strode up to me and hissed angrily, but the others in the restaurant told Misery to stop troubling me and to accept her defeat graciously, and she was fed the largest fish on the menu that night for her part in the performance.

25

SLEEPING BEAUTY

We had a bet, the damsel and I.

I told her she wouldn't be able to spend a night in the room without being tempted to get into that bed at least once.

She admitted the bed was indeed the most beautiful she had ever laid eyes on and that the temptation to sink into it would no doubt be almost impossible to resist. *Almost impossible*, she reiterated. *But not entirely out of the question.*

We agreed that she would take up lodgings in the room for free for an entire year were I to lose the bet.

And if at any time of the night I caught her wrapped under the covers for a bit of shut-eye, she would pay me twice the asking amount in rent for a year.

And so she turned up last evening at sundown, two books in one hand and a carton of clove-flavoured cigarettes in the other. *To keep me company all night,* she said. I made her three pots of tea so she wouldn't go pottering about in the rest of the house in the dead of the night.

When I finally shut the bedroom door behind her last

evening, the leaves of the apple trees had begun to sing their lullabies in rustles and whispers.

I went to check on her shortly before breakfast this morning.

She was gone.

The room was mostly as empty and as pristine as it had been before she arrived last evening. A cosy fug of clove and apple scents pressed upon me as I entered. I threw open the curtains; a little sunshine would dispel the odour in no time. Three empty pots of tea rested on the bedside table; I would clean them in time for the next visitor. The bed had been made; it likes to do that itself.

I have never tried to find out what goes on in the room at night. The previous owner of the house had once told me that the damsels fall into eternal slumber when they get into the bed, and disappear from this world. Only their Prince Charmings would be able to find them and kiss them to wakefulness.

But I don't see how that is going to happen; men are not permitted to take up lodgings here.

But mine is not to question and ponder. I cast a quick glance around the room. Everything seems to be in order.

Two Erin Morgenstern paperbacks lie on the floor. I pick these to add them to my collection of left-behinds on the mantelpiece in the living room downstairs. I like guests who leave behind useful things.

26

HOPE

*I*f you want to talk to the hornbills, you will find them at the usual place at the usual time.

It is breeding season. The females have locked themselves away in their nests, where they will remain for a few months laying their eggs and caring for their young.

The males are busy hunting for food, feeding their women, worrying about the next command that will be hurled at them, and snatching precious moments of time to work on their secret project.

A surprise for the girls and the little ones, the leader of the clan declares.

The male hornbills spend their stolen moments of time burrowing away underground in the centre of their mammoth cage.

Each day they start digging close to noon and keep at it for an hour, taking care to finish before the caretakers of the bird park return from their lunch to check on the birds.

Often they continue digging at night, noiselessly in the

dark. When the birds call it a day, the creeper plants reposition themselves to hide the entrance to the secret tunnel.

At first they don't want to talk about it, the birds that is. But once they are convinced we mean them no harm, they break into a ceaseless chatter.

The tunnel is to be their means of escape from the cage, they say.

Progress is excruciatingly slow, they admit but they remain hopeful.

Getting closer to freedom, they keep telling themselves.

Our children will learn to crawl before they learn to fly, one of the clan chuckles.

They want to leave so their children can learn to fly in the free skies, they explain.

Learn to hunt for food, fight their enemies, build their own nests. Things they can't learn growing up in a cage, they say.

We ask them why they wouldn't consider flying away as an option. They say their children will be too young and their women too weak to fly far.

And how long would it take them to dig the tunnel to the other end of the world?

They have been digging for five years now. Another six months, a year, maybe two at most, who knows. They hope to keep digging for as long as it takes them to make good their escape.

And they quote from the movies to prove they are not off their rockers. (They have seen all the good movies, they assure us.)

Some birds are not meant to be caged, that's all, one says.

Hope is a good thing, another chips in, *maybe the best of things, and no good thing ever dies.*

We think it is impossible to argue against conviction that strong.

27

THE TELEPHONE BOOTH

It is a plain-looking telephone. So although it has been placed in a cosy corner (and someone has thoughtfully set down a vase of orchids beside it) with a grand entrance announcing its presence and availability, the telephone remains mostly unused. The busy people zip along the corridor without so much as a second glance at the little black device.

An emergency, and a smart but dead phone made me step into the telephone booth and pick up the receiver. I stuck out my forefinger to jab at the numbers that made up my mother's phone number. (I am proud to say I have an acute memory for phone numbers; the increasing ability of inanimate objects to remember and repeat has not eroded my memory.)

Only there were no buttons on the dial pad. No numbers to dial. Where the dial pad ought to have been was a smokescreen, tendrils of white mist and rainbow colours swimming beneath the surface as if in a crystal ball. I held the receiver to my ear; that seemed to be the only thing to do.

Hello, crooned a voice so rich it seemed to spill warm golden sunlight on me. It asked me where I wanted to go and I said that I had no plans to go anywhere and that I was only trying to place a phone call but that there was no dial pad on this device, which is strange, I added, because it says *Telephone* at the entrance and of what use is a telephone without a dial pad, I asked.

The voice, which seemed to come from nowhere near but from all around me at the same time, enveloped me in a warm cocoon and said it was sorry to hear of my ordeal. And in order to compensate me for the trouble I've had to face, it offered to arrange for me to visit the person I was trying to place a call to. All expenses paid, it added.

I said that was very kind indeed and that I would love that very much.

Very well, Ma'am, said the voice, and with a clap and a poof I was gone and reappeared at the gate to my parents' house.

I find it is a useful thing, this inconspicuous telephone. So far, at my bidding, it has sent me on little jaunts to many places across the globe. But time travel is beyond its capabilities, it says. It is unable send me to a past or a future where telephones do not exist, for the simple reason that I wouldn't be able to return to the present, it explains.

~

28

THE BOY IN THE CLOUD

The boy in the cloud tells you it is a fairly easy climb. It only appears difficult because people (adults that is) generally do not take enthusiastically to such endeavours, climbing one step at a time surely but steadily, heading upwards one rung at a time. And because many people in general do not take to such endeavours enthusiastically, it only appears difficult.

Understandably, you can't quite grasp his logic and tell him as much.

He says it is a vicious cycle, the kind that keeps going in a loop such that you forget where it started and can't figure out where it is supposed to end.

He makes no sense, so you keep mum, not wanting to sound thickheaded again.

He watches you keenly for a while. Your fingers cross and uncross themselves in the depths of your pockets while the rest of you stands taut.

"A penny for your thoughts," he throws the bait.

"Give me a penny first," you say.

"Give me your thoughts first," comes the reply.

Only he manages to make it sound like a command and you are sure you had sounded like Oliver Twist.

"Alright," you concede. "I was thinking that you were merely trying to trap me in wordplay. All that talk of vicious cycles and repeating a sentence backwards to make it appear as if you had uttered two entirely different sentences in the breath of one. I think you are ..." You pause. He is too young for profanities.

"Go ahead, spit it out," he challenges you. "You think I am what? Bullshitting you?"

"I didn't say it," you promptly go on the defensive, sensing those scarlet eyes boring into yours, his thoughts and yours bridging the great distance between the two of you, pulling you closer to him while also tearing you apart.

His lips are pursed. The blood-red eyes are incongruous on the cherub face of the little child. Incredible. Because the harder your look, the more you realize the face is yours, from all those years ago.

"You could prove me wrong, you know," he teases. "Grab the rope, climb up, and let your legs dangle over the edge."

You hesitate.

"It is a nice feeling, you'll see," he promises.

The air around you shifts as if it were trying to dispel your doubts.

You stumble forward, warily at first, and as the rope comes into greater focus, the clarity lifts your spirits. You break into a run, feeling light as a feather. When you near the rope, you leap and grab it with both hands and begin your upward scramble, lifting your weightless self effortlessly, buoyed by the newfound strength in your arms. Rung after rung you clamber up.

And when you reach the top, you are near enough to see the boy smiling. Rather evilly. As if he has just pulled a fast one on you and you proved an easy prey. He stretches one arm towards yours as if to pull you over the last rung and onto the ring of cloud.

Even as he does, his flaming red eyes dissolve into a black emptiness. Lines of age bite deep into the virgin skin of his face and hands. His puckered lips crack at the edges and fade from a moist pink to an ashen lifelessness. His tender locks of hair evaporate into the air and the few strands that remain are a spectral grey-white.

As you see yourself age seven decades in an instant, the boy — now an unrecognizable assemblage of withered flesh and old bones — leans over to you and says, "I have no pennies to spare," and shoves you over the edge.

You make a grab at the rope but all your manage to grasp is a handful of airy emptiness.

And you fall.

Endlessly.

Limbs flailing.

The lightness of your being as you sprinted towards the rope is now replaced with a solid heaviness that drags you down with such force you are certain it emanates from within you, from the depths of your chest.

Your heart beats incessantly like the flapping wings of a hummingbird, so rapid it appears still.

Bells toll in the distance. A funeral, you wonder. Perhaps yours?

You wish the bells would stop. The racket is now inside your head, growing worse than the pounding in your chest.

You cannot bear it any longer.

You know your heart is about to explode and cover what remains of you in a million broken pieces.

You squeeze your eyes shut.

You are forced to surrender.

Your body strikes the hard ground and you crumble into lifelessness.

And you wake up in another world.

As you slam the alarm shut, you think you will be late for work again today. You have a fleeting thought, something to do with bad pennies, but before you can consider it, it slithers away into the realms of the unconscious, forever out of your reach.

~

29

THE GOLDEN BOY

The golden boy sat by the stream, his gaze fixed longingly upon the waters prancing and rollicking past. It appeared to me he wanted to take a dip without running the risk of having the colour washed away from him. As with everything unusual, I was mistaken.

He said he did indeed long for a dip but he did in fact want the yellow to be washed off. But the water was blue and he did not want to turn blue.

I tried to convince him that water had no colour in it and that it appeared blue only because it stole the blue from the sky sometimes, usually when it felt drab and colourless.

At that he began to worry that a dip in the stream would leave him drab and colourless. And the thought conjured up in his mind the notion of invisibility. His voice quivered. He did not want to vanish from the world, he stressed.

I asked him what his favourite colour was and whether I could paint that over the yellow. He shook his head sadly and said that right now his favourite colour was the colour of skin, and that he could not recall having ever liked any colour more than how much he now longed for the colour of skin.

I asked him how he had turned yellow and he said a little yellow girl had kissed him. Mother had warned him about the faeries of the forest and had forbidden him from playing with the colourful kids, he cried quietly.

I could not think of anything else to say or do, so I offered to give him the colour of my skin in exchange for his. At that the boy leapt up in delight and hugged me with a wrap of his arms around my legs, so tiny was he. I buried my face in his hair. The thick unruly but fleecy locks of the little child caressed my cheeks. The scent of lavender and lemongrass filled my being.

When we pulled away from each other, I could see he was transformed into a rubescent cherub. My hands and legs were as flaxen as my tresses.

The boy thanked me and gambolled away into the meadows.

I sit by the stream wondering whether someone would come along to my rescue. How long would it take, I wonder. I think I will bathe in the stream. I am not sure if it will simply wash away the yellow or turn me blue in the process. Or render me invisible. What if the stream turned yellow?

30

MIDNIGHT MISCHIEF

*T*he crescent moon hung in the inky sky like an unfulfilled promise.

She cast a dull silvery glow on the forestland that lay sprawled at her feet, no more than an endless clump of interfused silhouettes at this time of the night.

A gentle breeze rustled the leaves, and their whispers and susurrations travelled urgently to the far ends of the forest.

Two little heads peeped shyly out of the hollow at the base of the oldest eucalyptus in the forest — a three thousand-year old resident of the woods well-versed in the ways of children and only too happy to abet mischief-makers and trouble-seekers.

The boys — no older than five and seven — hesitated.

The eucalyptus stirred and with a stray root gave the lads a little flick each on their backs.

"Off you run, you two," the tree bid.

"Ow," yelped the little one.

"Thank you, Mr. Eucalyptus," said the older one with more composure than his slightly sore back would permit.

The boys tiptoed through the forest as quietly as they could, which, to tell the truth, turned out to be a very noisy affair and would have scared away the moon, the older boy admonished the younger one en route.

But they made it without incident to their destination — the edge of a clearing secretly tucked away in the folds of the forest. They abandoned the camouflage of the trees and stepped into the clearing together, then looked up longingly at the moon.

"Could we play tonight?" they beseeched her.

No response came their way.

"Could we play tonight?" they implored once more.

She opened one eye lazily and muttered, "Manners."

"Could we please please please play tonight?" the little voices chorused.

The moon let out a languorous sigh at first.

But unable to conceal her pleasure for much longer, she puffed out her cheeks and billowed out like a balloon into a perfectly rotund shape that adorned the sky as its centrepiece.

Under her argent watch, a little centaur and a tinier unicorn frisked and frolicked in the clearing all night.

31

STRINGING WISHES ON A TREE

$\mathcal{E}$very evening, the girl who lives in the house at the end of the lane hangs lanterns of twinkling candles from the branches of the oak tree in her garden. It looks like a fun thing to do. And she seems like a lovely girl. So when I turn up at her doorstep, eager to be part of the ritual, she gladly agrees to teach me how to make and put up lanterns on her oak tree.

It doesn't take long to figure that making the lantern is the easiest bit. The tricky part is the getting the right ingredients for it.

The first thing you will need, she says, is a jar of glass. A jar old enough to hold a story, she stresses.

Next, a handful of pebbles that bring back a wonderful memory.

And finally, a scent you wish to forget, she concludes.

The next evening I show up at her doorstep, my loot in my hands.

A little jar that had once held the hearts of all my loved

ones. I found it in the toolshed, forgotten and cloaked in a thick blanket of dust.

The pebbles, Hummer fetched for me.

One by one.

Choosing each one meticulously.

It took him all afternoon.

But when he will be gone and I will have grown too old and forgetful, the pebbles will remind me of his warm fur.

The pebbles fill my jar halfway.

The girl plants a candle in the centre. She then turns to me and asks me to light the candle with the fragrance I wish to forget.

I put my lips to the brim of the jar and gently blow on to the wick of the candle. A hiss and a spark and the candle bursts into life. The girl looks at me curiously. The scent of a lost lover's kiss, I answer her unvoiced question.

She smiles and loops a string around the neck of my jar.

You could wish for anything you know, she confides, when you hang the lantern.

Anything? I ask.

She nods.

What do you usually wish for? I ask her.

Every evening, she says, I wish for the lights to show me the way long after I have run out of stars and dreams.

I take a cue from her and wish for hope and strength to last me long after I have run out of loved ones.

32

EN ROUTE TO THE SUN

The path leading to the sun is straight, which, in my opinion, is a little strange. I would have expected it to be littered with obstacles and dead-ends and little side streets that appear to be shortcuts but really end up leading you nowhere close to the destination.

But no, not this one. No twists and turns. No hairpin bends. It is straight as the truth.

For some reason, it seems right to walk single file, and so we do. When we reach the end of the pier, the path leading to the sun ends abruptly. The ocean lies sprawled at our feet, its waters shimmering like diamonds on fire.

The old man says we are ill-equipped to cross the ocean to reach the sun, and that it is best to turn back. His wife nods in agreement and they walk back single file, she stepping into his footsteps.

The young man thinks it is a shame to give up after having come thus far. So he decides to build a boat that would take him across the ocean. And so he turns back, planning to head back into the forest for wood.

The little girl sits by the edge of the pier and dips her feet in the water. She calls out to the mermaids who say they'd ferry her across but only if she sings for them. And off she goes.

Caramel suggests we try to leap across. I am skeptical at first but he keeps tugging at his leash. He puts a paw over the edge and a fragment of a bridge appears under his foot. He steps on it and puts another paw over the edge. And more of the bridge comes into view wherever he intends to step. And that is how we skip all the way to the sun, one sure step at a time.

When we look back, the bridge has disappeared, as if it had never existed. Caramel tells me to not worry. *We will find it again when we need it*, he assures me.

33

I AM SORRY. I DO NOT HAVE A STORY FOR TODAY.

I am sorry.

I do not have a story for today.

I am sorry.

But I have already said that, that I am sorry.

(There I go again!)

The truth is, I did have a story to begin with.

A nice, succulent tale that twists and turns and coils and uncoils itself, sometimes with the beauty of Rapunzel's golden braids, at other times with the sinuousness of serpents. A story with a well-defined beginning, a distinct middle, and an incontrovertible end. The kind that stays with you, as a good friend does, long long after it has been read and forgotten.

I unearthed the story from a little burrow under the hedge that separates our garden from the rest of the world. (I had often seen Caramel digging there furiously, making himself a neat little hideout to nestle in on a lazy afternoon. I had always assumed it was a bone he had hidden there. One day I saw it (that which I had assumed was a bone) move and whisper and sing and dance and quiver in the wind, and it was when I went to take a look that I discovered what it really was. A tale waiting to be told.)

I scooped the tale into a little jar I had meant to keep butterflies in, but the tale was just as beautiful and flitted about in the jar just as prettily. And I set out on a journey from my home in the middle of the garden on the edge of the rest of the world, so I could bring the tale to you.

From all the stories I had read until then, I knew all there was to know about the seven mountains and the seven seas. And so I had no unforeseen difficulty traversing them. But after I crossed the seventh sea and stepped onto its shores, a little path led me up a river to a little wooden bridge over it.

Under the bridge stood a troll, who appeared as if he had been waiting for me. When I approached him, he said he was pleased to see me but unhappy to learn of his portrayal as an ugly, dim-witted, thieving creature in the story I carried in my jar.

And because he gave me such a piteous look, which was unbecoming for a troll, I held out my jar and he took the story in his clumsy fingers and gave it a little pinch here and a tiny bend there, then put it back in the container and lidded it and handed it back to me.

When I asked what he had done, he said the troll in the story was now a different character, one that helps the Little Prince cross the bridge instead of trying to kill him.

I crossed the bridge, leaving behind a happy troll, only to find an unhappy Little Prince waiting for me on the other side. He leapt out at me brandishing a sword, demanding to know why I had let the shape of the story be changed. I recounted to him my encounter with the troll under the bridge.

The Little Prince pointed his sword at my chest, and growled that because the troll's life had now been spared in the story, he (the Little Prince) would have to kill someone else as the prophecy would otherwise remain unfulfilled.

I thought the Little Prince meant he was about to chop my head off, instead he grabbed the jar, let the story out, and gave it a snip here and a nick there and handed back the jar to me.

I did not stay to ask what he had done, instead I ran into the woods as fast as my legs could take me without my heart exploding, stopping only when I realized I had come too far and no longer knew where I was, where I was headed, where I had come from.

I began to panic, but soon fear gave way to relief when a little fairy appeared from nowhere and hovered above me. I wanted to ask her if she could get me out of the forest and take me to you safely, but as she glided nearer, I could see she was crying.

She said the Little Prince had killed her in the tale in my jar because the troll had tricked me into sparing his life. And she said she was crying not so much because she was killed but because she is required in a later chapter where she saves the Little Prince from the clutches of an evil witch, but now that he has killed her in an earlier chapter she couldn't see how she was going to fulfil that role anymore. And of what use is a story if good did not prevail over bad in the end?

I held the jar out to the fairy, she sprinkled some stardust into it, and the story shimmered and sparkled and luminesced like coloured powder on a butterfly's wings. She told me to head east until I found an oak tree that would tell me what to do next.

I reached the oak tree not too long after. But my legs

buckled and I sank beneath the tree. And where there was earth only moments ago, was suddenly now a hole that grew larger and larger by the instant, and sucked me inside it.

I fell through the hole, and I kept falling, endlessly it seemed, and I fell some more, not like a comet hurtling from outer space but like a feather gliding, biding its time, guided by a gentle breeze. And when I landed, it was like coming to rest in slow motion on a feather bed. Only, the bed was severely undersized, large enough for me to barely rest my right leg on it.

And it was there that I found Alice, large and oversized, like a big child who had somehow found her way into her favourite dollhouse and figured it wasn't as comfortable and fun on the inside as it had appeared from the outside.

I asked her if she could help me get out of there and she said there was only one way out. And she put her hands over my face and closed my eyes and I drifted into a deep sleep.

When I opened my eyes next, I found myself by the little burrow under the hedge that separated our garden from the rest of the world.

The sun shone in my eyes, Caramel lay in the burrow chewing on his bone, and in a little jar beside us a butterfly fluttered, the colours on its wings stolen from the far corners of the earth.

Caramel nudged me and I uncovered the jar. The butterfly landed on my cheek for a fleeting second, then darted to land on Caramel's wet nose, and flew away into the sunlight. And with it, took the story I wanted to share with you.

And so I am sorry. I do not have a story for today.

~

34

A CINDERELLA TALE

When she received an invitation to the ball, Cinderella scurried about the house looking for all the things she would need before her fairy godmother arrived at dusk.

Cobwebs spun by twelve-legged spiders would be woven into a fine gossamer dress for her to wear that evening.

One large pumpkin she had stolen from her neighbour's garden last Halloween (although she couldn't remember how) would become the coach to take her to the ball.

She wasn't particularly fond of mice, so she thought she would instead ask the white doves to draw her coach.

We could transform the stepsisters into horses and make them draw the coach, a little voice piped up.

Cinderella shushed the voice and busied herself in her household chores.

Think about it, continued the voice. *The stepmother would make a fine coachman, seeing as how good she is at using the whip.*

Cinderella ignored it, and dusted the furniture.

What if the pumpkin is all rotten from the inside and the coach collapses as soon you step on it?

Cinderella shut out the truth of possibility, and swept and mopped the floors.

What if the fairy godmother doesn't turn up?

Cinderella told the voice to shut up, and did the dishes.

What if the prince already has a lover leaning on his arms?

Cinderella sang aloud, and washed the clothes and hung them out to dry.

When evening came and her stepsisters and stepmother left for the ball, Cinderella ran up to the attic to wait. Evening bled into night but no one came. Cinderella started to sob at the realization that she was doomed to a life of eternal slavery, and that there was no happy ending in store for her.

Look, said the voice. *You tried it your way and it didn't work. You might as well let me have a go at it now.*

Cinderella kept mum. And as suddenly as grey clouds conquer a clear sky, she stood up and shook herself. She wiped the tears with the back of her hands, landed a swift kick at the pumpkin and sent it hurtling down the stairs, and tore through the house once more like a whirlwind. She picked a rucksack from one of her stepsisters' room and filled it with good clothes, sensible shoes, and loads of money from her stepmother's wallet, and slipped out of the house.

The stepsisters and stepmother returned home to find a note from Cinderella saying she was gone and that she had paid herself in cash and kind for all the household services she had rendered all these years.

The note also carried a warning against reporting the incident to the police or attempting to track her as she would then be compelled to produce proof of how her father's death had come about at the hands of her stepmother.

She is writing a book now, titled *Cinderella and I*, recounting her escape and subsequent adventures across the world.

~

Preface to "Cinderella and I"

I am sorry to break this to the world but Cinderella was damaged goods. Who wouldn't be after years of domestic abuse? She needed someone to look after her, someone real, not illusory figures like Prince Charming or fairy godmothers or some such fantastic figment of imagination.

I am happy to say Cinderella is well and recovering now, under my careful oversight and guidance, though she keeps mostly to herself these days.

The miracle was that she found it within herself to bring about the transformation. As her closest friend and ally, I am honoured she considers me her true voice and has given me this opportunity to present her story, our story, to the world.

~ The Voice

~

35

UNDERWATER GODS

Not all gods live in the heavens.

Countless have their abodes on earth.

Some others are banished to underwater depths, where no living creature, whether with or devoid of faith, knows to pray.

The Earth Gods largely outnumber the Sky Gods.

The latter are understandably the most sought after and people always look up to the heavens when they remember God.

The former are so many in number and so commonplace now that people have had to pick favourites; which gods grant their wishes and which don't, which ones are reputed for speedy answers to their prayers and which ones aren't.

But not many know about the Underwater Gods.

Sometimes a diver or two loses his way in the waters and wanders into the cathedral. Often he returns with a cast of hundreds, and the cathedral is photographed and marvelled upon. Replicas are built on land, stories of faith are woven around it, and tourists pause to be overwhelmed by the possibility of underwater worship.

Sometimes people go down in search of God. Usually they end up being distracted by the dazzling colours of underwater life and return to the surface believing they have found God.

Whenever there are visitors, the gods freeze themselves into little statues adorning the arches of the cathedral. They make no sound, no movement, and hold their breath until the visitors have left.

If you ask them, they'd tell you discomfort is the little price they pay to preserve their privacy. They know that if they remain hidden, people will soon stop looking for them.

36

THE DECADE OF SEASONS

Summer that decade lasted two and a half years.

It was the season of the fiercest parching heat.

Flowers wilted.

Crops parched.

Vineyards shrivelled up.

Leaves dried up and crumpled to the touch like old paper.

Birdsong faded like a distant memory.

Oceans dried up, seabeds served as mass graves.

The earth ruptured and fissured, and began to crumble.

But everyone remembered it as the summer that mermaids disappeared from the face of the earth.

When the rains finally came, they lasted merely a month.

That was all the time the skies needed.

As if the heat had burnt up the skies and there was nothing to hold back the downpours.

What the heat did not destroy, the rains demolished.

The waters filled up the cracks in the earth, oceans and rivers swelled to life and transgressed whatever boundaries may have once existed.

When they were convinced it was finally safe, the mermaids rose from their groundwater havens and swam to the surface.

They looked around but there was no land to be found.

And there was no one to remark this was the monsoon that brought the mermaids back to life.

37

CONVERSATIONS

The thing I miss the most about us is our conversations.

Our frequent rendezvous at the coffee shop where we discussed dreams and drew up plans for the future.

Moonlight trysts and the ghost stories you used to spin, knowing how much they terrified me. And despite all my outward protestations of fear I had a secret longing to be terror-struck, and you knew that, and that, your knowing, is something I miss too.

The conversations at the park bench after a morning run, our breaths frosting in the cold winter air as you whispered sweet nothings in my ear.

The late-night telephone chats when you were continents away. Words that travelled across time and space, their meanings sometimes failing to keep pace, but the words always stayed with me long after we hung up and went about our separate lives.

Then the I do's.

And not long after, the I don't want to's.

And then there were the things left unsaid but more real than spoken words. They hung between us in an invisible bubble that kept us apart and grew larger and larger as more and more things were left unsaid.

And now you are gone.

And I can't remember your voice anymore.

And all that remain are the voices in my head.

38

THE TRAIL OF THE YELLOW
SYCAMORE LEAVES

When we first set out on an expedition to the far end of the world, the wise old man who lives at the edge of the forest advised us to stick to the trail of the yellow sycamore leaves.

And he told us to hurry because autumn was swiftly coming to an end and winter was lurking around the corner.

We scrambled through the forest but the paths were cloaked in a million shades of red. Flaming oranges bled into raging vermilions. Flamboyant auburns mellowed into rose or were devoured by incensed scarlets.

We turned over each leaf looking for traces of yellow, but in vain.

The last of the leaves soon deserted the trees, which were left to stand in naked silence. And the snow, when it fell, buried the last vestiges of colour.

When winter had had his fill and spring breezed her way through the forest, we set out once more on the well-trodden and offbeat trails. The paths were clean and clear.

The trees that had once drooped under the weight of winter, pulled back to stand tall and strong to support their nascent canopies of green. There was no sign of the yellow sycamore leaves.

Summer came and the forest was drenched in the golden warmth of the sun. The trees rose higher to kiss the sun. The only leaves that drifted earthwards were brown as mud and dry as twigs.

Summer's liaison with the forest ended when winter started to get impatient and sent autumn ahead to pave the way for him.

Summer bade the forest farewell and the sun-kissed leaves started to turn yellow in fond remembrance.

When it became clear summer wasn't returning for another year, the yellow sycamore leaves floated away from the trees and drifted deep over the earth, where they formed a path they hoped would lead them to the sun.

We plough through the forest a third time, on the trail of the yellow leaves, making haste this time before the leaves decide to turn an infuriated red.

Miles after miles of forestland lie blanketed in yellow leaves. The scenery changes little and often we think we are going around in circles.

But we do reach the far end of the world and the only way we know it is because there is no more land for the yellow leaves to lay their trail.

They converge at the end and rise up, coiling themselves into what looks like a helical staircase leading up into the clouds.

They say they are going up the meet the sun and that we could continue to travel with them if we want to.

We are not sure what to do.

A trip to the sun sounds fun.

But we think the yellow leaves shouldn't be trusted. We still do not know their true colours.

39

WHEN THE GHOSTS DO NOT COME CALLING

For several years after our parents died, my sister and I walked to the end of the pier every evening to read the message on the illuminated board installed in the middle of the ocean.

She believed the messages that flashed on the board came from the afterworld. She also believed mum and dad would send us messages, and she didn't want to miss the communications when they arrived. I did not share her beliefs but I rarely let her walk alone.

Once I asked her what kind of messages she expected them to send. She simply shrugged and said she didn't know.

Perhaps a note saying they have arrived safely.

Arrived where? I asked.

Heaven, maybe? she reckoned, unwilling to entertain any other possibilities.

Some evenings I was unable to leave from work early enough to accompany her on her walks. On such days, she would set out by herself and sit at the end of the pier, staring unblinkingly at the board until I came by to bring her back home.

Maybe you should let them go, I said one evening. *Not hold them back.*

She disagreed, even though she was soaking wet and shivering in the rain that day. *I just want to know they are still out there. Somewhere,* she insisted.

The message on the metallic board has changed not once in the all the years we've been here.

I can no longer join my sister on her evening walks.

She hasn't stopped looking for mum and dad, but now she pins all her hopes on me.

Sometimes she calls out into the wind asking me to send her a message if I can hear her.

I watch her mutely. I wish there was something I could say or do to help her move on.

But there are some boundaries we simply must not transgress.

40

A HAPPY PLACE

And I say to him I am afraid I can't put up with it anymore. And he gives me a half-bored, half-quizzical, half-I-know-where-this-is-leading look. (I know I have put three halves in there and that such a thing is logically not possible but that is hardly the point and he knows better than to argue about that right now.)

And he also knows that the thing I think I simply cannot put up with anymore has nothing to do with him. I am only scared the well may have run dry and that I may have not a single story left in me and that I don't want to turn to the big, bad world out there for inspiration because it is a world filled with mean people who do not believe in stories and fairness, I sob to him.

And so he says he will take me to a place where all my miseries (both real and imagined, he mocks) and all of the world's problems will disappear.

He blindfolds me and leads me through many places and, like a tour guide, he keeps up a commentary on the destination as we go. But as far as I am concerned the only thing that appears real to me right now is that I am stumbling through a dark, unlit passage that seems to never end, and I fervently pray he never lets go of my hand.

It is a forgotten place, he says, the place he is leading me to. People know it exists but no one really remembers it does. Like houses not lived in for centuries. No one ever goes in or out. But if you look hard enough, you will see lights shining from the windows as if the house were having its own personal sunrise after the rest of the world has turned in for the night, he says.

I am walking more steadily now, my hand in his, and I trust he will keep me from falling as I lose myself in his narration. He asks me what I'd like to see when I reach there, this forgotten place.

I am beginning to like the game he is playing, and so I play along and answer *fairy lights*. He says I will not be disappointed.

A few steps ahead, he slows down and reveals this is as far as he can go but that I must carry on. Only a few more steps, he insists.

I hesitate at first but having come this far I do not want to return without knowing where it was we were headed in the first place.

I push ahead, guided by my senses now there is no storyteller to lead me on the path. The air is crisp and wintry. I hear the leaves and twigs crack under my feet. Night creatures are playing their music and singing their songs, and I don't feel lonely. I keep thinking of the fairy lights I want to see.

When I know I have arrived, I pull away the blindfold and open my eyes. I see a million tiny lights floating all around me. Little green pinpricks of light shining, gliding, disappearing, then reappearing elsewhere in the dark, as if bobbing about to the music of the creatures of the night.

I turn to tell him I know where I am.

I know this is my happy place.

41

THE WEDDING OF THE TIN SOLDIER AND THE PAPER BALLERINA

*D*ear Santa,

After years of simply loving her from a distance, the tin soldier has finally asked the paper ballerina out and the two of them are quite the couple now.

Happiest about this is the cat who has been practising playing the fiddle and he intends to give what he hopes would be a stellar performance when the wedding bells ring next year.

We intend to invite Her Most Gracious Majesty and we hope she will grace us with her presence at the wedding but the ballerina is worried that a last-minute incident could prevent the royalty from attending, and so she insisted on having a backup. So the frog has been practising hard at shape-shifting and she can now turn into a gorgeous princess at the snap of a finger.

We do have a (real) princess in our midst but she has been very upset that the tin soldier fell in love with the ballerina and not with her. We think it would be cruel to invite her to the wedding. But that is not to say she is bitter about it all.

She has promised to stitch dresses for all of us to wear to the wedding.

But she has also secretly planned to leave town the night before the wedding, and the cow has promised he will let her ride on his back that night as he jumps over the moon. They say there is a man on the moon waiting for her.

And all this, we promise, will be no trouble at all to the family that lives in the house. We do not really know who they are for during the day we lie quietly on top of one another in the dusty, old shoe-box tucked under silver-grey cobwebs in the darkest corner of the forgotten cupboard under the rickety stairs. We troop out only at night after everyone has fallen asleep and slip back into the shoebox without a noise before the first light of dawn.

The only trouble is the tin soldier and the ballerina have no other home to go to after their wedding. So, dear Santa, when you sail through the chimney this December, could you please gift them a doll-house this Christmas?

Yours obediently,
The Blue Doll

42

THE LITTLE MUSE WHO LIVES IN THE TYPEWRITER

Master had instructed me to never enter his study.

The day I first showed up for work at the manor, he said I was to clean and tidy up the whole house everyday but that his study was strictly out of bounds.

And that of course means I have snooped around the study on every occasion that has since presented itself to me innocuously.

My first few visits were mostly uneventful. It is a lovely study, no doubt. Shelves of beautiful books run up the walls. The French windows on the far end open onto a vast garden that gives way to sprawling meadows cloaked in a million shades of green, unfolding lazily to kiss the horizon.

Master's desk sits in the centre of the room, buried under reams of paper, holding a typewriter, an eclectic collection of pens and pencils scattered haphazardly on the desk, and sundry other items.

I sometimes read through the pages and wonder aloud

how such lousy prose could earn Master his reputation as a famed connoisseur of tales.

It was only on my fourth or fifth visit did I discover the little muse who lives in the typewriter. She thinks my name is Psst because that is how she addresses me whenever she wants to grab my attention. I correct her each time but to no avail.

Often she asks me to fetch her a cup of lavender tea, and I do. It usually makes her happy.

In return, she shows me a few tricks. My favourite is the one in which she snaps her fingers and dances on the keys. And when she does that, the words on the pages on the desk start to tremble as if they are in an attempt to break free from the story that binds them.

And she shuffles and reshuffles and rearranges the words so that when I read Master's story again, it is no longer his because it is no longer a story and instead, it is now a tale converted into magic. Just as how his publisher would like it, the muse says.

I tell her he never acknowledges her contribution to his work.

And she nods in understanding and says that that is quite alright. As long as her stories are alive and well for all to savour, she says, it does not matter who claims to have written them.

43

THE UNKNOWN DESTINATIONS OF
PAPER AIRPLANES

Paper planes are easy to make. The hardest bit is getting them to fly.

The first time I flung one, it soared upwards, hit the ceiling, and nosedived to land on my right foot.

The first time I managed to fly one well enough was during Math class in third grade. The plane landed under Suzie's desk and tickled the nose of a little lizard that had been dozing there.

Shaken by the flying piece of paper, the lizard darted across the floor, leaped on to Suzie's lap, then on to her desk, and made a bolt for the wall but not before she let out a shriek that caused our teacher to faint and brought the teachers from all other classrooms rushing into ours.

And my paper plane lay innocuously under Suzie's desk as incontrovertible proof of my guilt. (No one believed my story of the lizard, and Suzie insisted there had never been one, though she did roll her eyes and stick her tongue out at me when she thought no one else was looking.)

Sometimes my planes flew up and got stuck in the branches of trees.

Sometimes they'd manage to get themselves snared in the jumble of electric wires atop tall poles.

Often they'd just somersault in place and fall on my head.

The only person I knew who knew how to make paper planes fly was my brother. And he refused to let me in on the secret.

For seven years he derived pleasure in watching my clumsy efforts and laughing at my futile attempts. And when he planned to move to the city (in search of a better life), I worried that with him, his secret too would be gone forever. But when he boarded the bus and turned to wave at us from the window, he looked at me and yelled that they need to be told where to go.

I have since figured there are many ways to guide the planes to their destinations.

Sometimes I just whisper to them before setting them on their way. Sometimes I scribble the names of places on them. My neighbour's rooftop, the haunted oak tree at the edge of the fields, as far as the summer wind will take them, into my lover's home, as high as the eagle soaring above the mountaintops, on the other side of the horizon.

I try to make bigger planes now. I hope some day they will be large enough for me to ride in them. And I will tell them to take me closer to you.

～

44

IN WHICH YOU ENCOUNTER ANGELS BANISHED FROM HEAVEN AND LOOKING FOR A PLACE TO LIVE ON EARTH

The angels admit they were banished from heaven but they will not reveal why.

Some say the angels must have done terrible things but the angels themselves neither confirm nor deny these rumours.

They (the angels) say very little, in fact.

They mostly stand at the market square all day, still as stone, so you can't even see their nostrils flare or their chests heave and you wonder whether they breathe. Or perhaps they are just cheap mannequins stationed to prey on the generosity of tender-hearted souls, you think.

And so you move closer to them, wondering whether or not you could glide the back of your hand over their smooth cheeks to determine if they are made of flesh or stone.

You finally muster up enough courage to hold your finger under their noses and feel their warm breaths tumble over your skin in unwavering rhythm and dissipate into the atmosphere.

You fish around in your pockets for a dollar or two but

come up with a handful of loose change, all that you've accumulated so far this month. And you are about to tip the coins into the jar but the angels say they have no use for your money.

You look up but they remain motionless. Their lips unmoving, their eyes looking vacantly into the distance.

Yet you can hear them speak. They tell you what they really need is a roof to live under, a place to call home, and ask if you would be so kind as to invite them into yours.

You shrug your shoulders and pretend to not have heard them. The coins feel uncomfortably heavy in your hand and you tip them noisily into the jar and walk away, mentally patting yourself on the back for having done your good deed for the day.

There is nothing more you can do, you tell yourself. After all, mother did teach you to not talk to strangers. And angels are no exception to the rule.

45

TREES ON A MISSION

The trees are in a hurry.

You can tell they have come a great distance from the way their trunks seem to have disappeared from under them, as if eroded from all the walking. Or gliding. Or dragging. Or whatever it is that trees do to get themselves from one place to another.

They know we are watching them, so they momentarily freeze in place. Innocuously, as if they have stood their ground all along. As if the visible absence of their trunks were some sort of nature's well-intended aberrations.

We ask them where they are headed but they maintain a stony silence.

The instant we look away, they shuffle forward.

Shuffling — that's the word! Shuffling is what trees do to get themselves from one place to another.

(Like determined old women tottering through memories to find the right one. Or like maidens in Elizabethan gowns skipping over moorlands in small steps, their feet searching for safe ground to step on amid the cascading folds of their skirts.)

We have been following them for days now.

We keep ourselves well out of sight, as otherwise the trees would halt and make no further progress.

Theirs is a noisy group, especially when they think no one's watching them. There is constant chatter amongst them and with other trees.

So far we have only caught a few words from their conversations — *war, the Dark One, danger, annihilation.*

We have also figured out that the trees can keep going only as long as they have enough leaves to keep up the momentum. When they fall short of leaves, they seek help from other trees en route, but they keep going.

They worry winter is fast approaching and soon there may not be enough leaves to go around. But if it comes to that, we think we can help by carrying them on our backs until spring arrives.

46

THROUGH THE LOOKING GLASS

They say if your bed faces a mirror, a part of your soul slips away from you and floats into the mirror when you are asleep at night. When I brought this up with the landlady, all she had to say was Balderdash!

She pointed out that they also say that were a black cat to cross your path, you were in for a lifetime of bad luck. And Tabby, her black cat, has been a lifetime companion to her and so far as she could tell, she had done pretty well for herself in life, she said with a sweeping motion of her arms to indicate the sprawling farm and the three-storeyed house with thirteen rooms that she owned.

She insisted all these were simply old wives' tales and also politely said she had no other rooms to let and nowhere else to put the mirror.

So I told myself that all the things they say are not necessarily true and paid the landlady a week's rent in advance.

The following morning, a piece of blue sky appeared in the mirror, although the skies outside were a heavy grey and raindrops haltingly trickled down the window behind the mirror.

The second morning, white clouds swam across my personal blue sky in the mirror.

On the third, a fiery little sun made its appearance in the glass and winked at me as I came out of the shower. I threw my towel over the mirror to keep out prying eyes.

By the end of the week, in the mirror had appeared tiny stars, a little angel, one grey cloud, and several colourful curlicues not unlike the twisted tangles of my hair.

I showed my landlady the mirror and told her these were all bits and pieces of my soul locked away in the looking glass.

At first she said she will never again dismiss everything they say. She then offered to let me take the mirror with me, in a gesture of redress, an offer I promptly took her upon as I didn't want to part with any piece of my soul.

She reckoned I must have a good soul, going by all the lovely little forms and shapes that have cropped up.

But, she added thoughtfully, that the true test of my goodness perhaps lay in what the characters in the mirror get up to when no one is looking.

47

───────

MONSTERS OF ALL KINDS ARE TO BE TRUSTED UNDER NO ACCOUNT

The little monster was dressed as a clown. In loud, bold colours and with a red bulbous nose to top it all. He insisted the nose was real and when I tried to yank it off, he howled, so I let go.

Granny said monsters, of all kinds, were to be trusted under absolutely no account.

But the clown and his pumpkin looked so tiny and pathetically harmless, I dismissed her warnings and asked him what brought him to our neighbourhood.

He said he has come to offer his services.

What kind of services? I asked.

He must have known somehow that I had little patience with children of any gender or size or age, for he offered to stand guard at our doorstep on Halloween and attend to the little imps that will make their customary call at our house that night yelling trick-or-treat.

I was only too happy to not have to repeatedly answer the door to the summons of pesky kids. But I also had enough good sense to ask him what kind of payment he sought for his proposed service.

He coughed and cleared his throat and said that the only payment he sought was in kind; chocolates to feed his little pumpkin, he said, patting the orange fruit on its head. I agreed. The pumpkin's toothy smile widened and it bounced up and down in a hideous display of happiness.

Silly as it may sound, I made the necessary arrangements to ensure a steady supply of confectioneries for the pumpkin, and left the clown and his fruit pet to their own devices. I did not see them again until Halloween when they reappeared at our doorstep.

The instant she saw them, Granny huffed and said monsters, of all kinds, were to be trusted under absolutely no account. I told her that this year we will not be troubled by demanding little imps knocking at our doors in the dead of the night. Even that did not assuage her. She only shook her head and said monsters, of all ... I tuned her out and returned to my chair by the window where I sat with a book on my lap.

When the first of the children came to our house, the clown caught their attention before they could reach for the door. He spoke in animated gestures but I could not hear what was being said.

Perhaps in response to what the clown said, the children then stuck their tiny hands into the pumpkin's mouth — presumably to grab their treats — when the pumpkin opened its mouth wide, as swiftly as ink blotting on paper, and in one sudden gulp swallowed the kids. The little children, there now, gone forever.

The following morning, I found the pumpkin had ensconced itself in our backyard. Whole and ripe, ready to be cut and cooked. No toothless grin. No hollow eyes. Just a harmless fruit. The clown was nowhere to be seen.

Granny said monsters, of all kinds, were to be trusted under absolutely no account, and bade me destroy the fruit. I tried hacking it to pieces, kicking it out, and even setting fire to the backyard.

When nothing worked, the clown's voice piped up out of nowhere, offering me his services.

Granny's words rang in my ears — monsters, of all kinds, are to be trusted under absolutely no account.

But this time, I truly have no choice.

48

REFLECTIONS

The little boy skipped through the forest as surefooted as someone who has been on the trail a thousand times blindfolded. I had to run to keep up with him.

He was leading me to the waters, so I paused for breath and drained the remaining drops of water from my canteen, but not without a second thought.

"Hurry up," he whooped from somewhere far ahead of me.

I stumbled after him, praying once again (to any God that cared to listen) that I wasn't being misled.

In my mind, I was convinced we were heading in the wrong direction.

The cave from where the waters had gushed forth relentlessly, we had long ago lost somewhere in the wilderness behind us. The boy had said the best water would be found downstream, and although he was merely a child, he lent a certain conviction to his words and I had found myself incapable of doubting him.

But that was then. Now, I realized that with each step forward, the roar of the waterfall had subsided imperceptibly. At first it had reduced to the gentle gurgling of a little stream, and then there had been the occasional swish of water lapping over pebbles. And even that had died away when I wasn't paying attention.

When I asked the boy about it, he said we had to leave all the noise behind and that the growing silence meant we were on the right path.

Now and then I hear the sound of a drop of water falling but we are so far away from the waters now I am convinced it's just the voices in my head playing tricks with my mind. We have come so far ahead now that even if I were to retrace my steps, I wouldn't be able to make it back alive.

Lost in these morbid thoughts I continued to plough ahead, head drooping so low in misery I didn't notice the little boy jumping up and down excitedly ahead of me nor did I hear him whisper out my name. He grabbed my hand when I reached him and pushed through a lump of overgrown weeds.

On the other side was water, clear as day and quieter than silence. It lay in a narrow pool that stretched endlessly up and down the forest. The water was so still it felt sacrosanct to disturb it, I thought for a fleeting instant, before putting my lips to its cool, shiny surface and hungrily swallowing it in huge mouthfuls.

Only when I was satiated did I lift my head and the waters returned to a stillness that did not seem incongruous to its nature.

It carried in it the reflections of the clear skies and snow-capped mountains, as if a whole other universe existed peacefully in its confines, mirroring the one above, so you couldn't tell which one was real and which was merely an echo.

I asked the little boy about it. And he said one was the other and vice versa too, so it didn't really matter which was which. Because, he explained, if you left the noise behind and stared long enough at your reflection, it would reveal your true soul.

49

THE WHIMSICAL DANCE OF SNOWBALLS IN TRANSIT

The snowballs flutter above the piles on the ground.

To a casual onlooker, it would appear as if they were rising from the ground, defying gravity, flying towards the skies.

Another would think the snowballs were falling gently, returning home, coming to rest on the piles below.

The little boy says the snowballs arch into a portal to another land.

His sister, the younger one, says she has seen fairies living inside the snowballs.

The elder sister says it is something like a mistletoe. You have to kiss your partner when you walk underneath the white archway, so you better be careful whom you choose to accompany you on a beautiful night.

Their mother says all her children are blessed with very active imaginations. Truth be told, she says, it is simply a creative being's imagination, an artist's creation. If you look closely enough you can see the blue-black threads of steel on which the snowballs are suspended. (But of course I won't go looking for them threads. You knew that, didn't you?)

The wise man asked me what I made of it all.

To me, I said, it appears like a moment frozen in time, caught between breaths, the snapshot of a dancer in motion.

Difficult to say whether they are still or in motion. If in motion, whether they are rising or falling.

Perhaps if we watched long enough, I imagine we would see the little globes of white floating up and down in little, gentle motions like the rise and fall of breath under the skin of our chests.

The wise man cackled with laughter and said that the snowballs kept up their whimsical dance to keep us trapped in our imaginary illusions, so we remain sufficiently distracted from the mischief that goes on beneath the harmless looking piles of snow, right under our noses.

50

THE MAN WHO FELL IN LOVE WITH THE MOON

"Legend has it that the man was banished to the moon for a crime he did not commit," Grandpa began, in that deep mysterious voice of his that made fidgety children sit still and listen to the story with rapt attention, even if they have heard the tale countless times before.

"Why Grumpa?" curious little Pippin piped up as always. "Why was he sent to the moon?"

"Because," Grandpa said slowly, "people are afraid of unknown, unfamiliar things. No one had been to the moon. Back in those days, she was still a strange, distant, unfamiliar land. People saw her only at night-time, and no one knew where she disappeared during the day. So they thought it was a lonely, terrifying place where unspeakable things could happen to you even during the day."

Grandpa wrapped his shawl a little tighter around him and huddled closer to the fireplace. A little shiver ran down our collective spines as we momentarily wondered about the unspeakable things that happened on the moon.

"But good things happen to good people," Grandpa assured us. "So when the man went to the moon, imagine his wonder when he found that the moon was in fact a lovely, little lady. A misunderstood lady, as she liked to refer to herself," he chuckled.

"Why Grumpa?" curious little Pippin piped up again. "Why misunderstood?"

The other children shushed him but Grandpa waved a hand to quieten them.

"Well, people have always believed it is the moon that drives people mad. They have always accused her of causing werewolves to emerge from hiding. The oceans turn restless at the sight of the moon, they say. They also claim she steals the light of the sun and calls it her own. And to this day many people continue to accuse the moon of all these wrongdoings," Grandpa huffed.

And then, as if some faraway memory had suddenly returned to him, his face creased into a million wrinkly smiles and he said, "But of course, it doesn't matter what people think. Because the man who went to the moon saw her for what she really was and fell in love with her."

"Did they marry, Grampa?" It wasn't curious little Pippin this time.

"Of course they did," Grandpa beamed.

"Did they live happily ever after, Grompa?" another not-Pippin chirped.

"Of course they do," Grandpa said. "But that is not where the story ends. Because you see, the man was banished to the moon for only two decades. When his sentence was over, he was summoned back to the earth. He pleaded with her to come with him to the earth, but her abode was in the skies and she begged him to not leave."

"But she is still up there in the skies," another little voice piped up.

"On most days, yes," Grandpa said.

"Does that mean he left her behind?"

"Yes and no," came Grandpa's reply. "It is true the moon couldn't leave the skies and the man had to make his way back to the earth. But when the man returned to earth, he brought back with him a small part of her. And he promised to visit her every night, which he did, and each morning when he returned he brought back a little part of her with him.

"With each passing night, the moon waned in the sky, a part of her having made its way to the man's abode on earth. So when it was new moon and the moon disappeared from the sky and the world barely gave a second thought as to where she had disappeared to, no one knew that the moon was playing in her lover's backyard, unknown to the rest of the world."

And this is how Grandpa always ended his story.

Sometimes one of the kids would ask him how he knew all this.

And if it were a new moon night, Grandpa would take us all into the backyard where the lovely moon would play with us until bed-time.

And in the cover of daylight, she would return to the skies, bit by bit, sliver by sliver over the course of a fortnight until she was a little globe of dreamy white again.

But what the little kids do not know is that Grandpa also leaves behind a part of him on the billowing moon after each visit.

There isn't much of him left on earth anymore. One day he will be gone for good.

And it will be up to me then to tell the children to look for him not among the stars but to seek out the man in the moon. I know the little ones will believe me.

51

THE LIGHT BY THE WINDOW

he house must have been over a hundred years old, fraying at the edges, corners crumbling quietly when no one was looking.

Every time we walked past, the sorry sight of the dilapidated home would grab us by the throat, and our eyes would scan the ramshackle building for the vestiges of the happy home that had disintegrated into debris.

At the same time something equally terrifying would make us quickly look away.

Nobody ever stepped into the grounds of overgrown weeds that circumscribed the house, but if we happened to walk past it at night-time, we could sometimes see a little warm globule of light shining warmly in the opaque blackness of the night.

People in the village mostly thought it was a little orb of a long-forgotten spirit. Better avoided than confronted, they said.

It was useful, that light, even if the sight of it meant we had to walk away from it, and not towards it.

I sometimes like to think it served as a beacon for lost souls.

52

IN SEARCH OF WINTER

When summer overstayed his welcome and winter showed no sign of making an appearance (and oh! autumn had all but disappeared from the face of this part of the earth), the locals blamed it on global warming and other newfangled terms that the Old Folk insisted were never in existence in the good old days.

Granny was one of the Old Folk and although I don't believe everything they say, I do believe everything she says.

So when she said yes, climate and weather were rarely capricious back in those times, I believed her.

And when she also said that we could still use some age-old wisdom to tame the elements to do our bidding, if only temporarily, I believed that too.

She sent me back in time to search for the good winters.

I was to look for the good old days and the good old nights cloaked in thick blankets of snow, cut them from the fabric of time, and weave them into the realm of the present day.

A swift snip here, a neat nick there, then stitch together

the snippets of time to form a patchwork of cold, wintry days.

I must have done a good job for Granny was pleased when I came back home, winter at my heels.

Winter, when she came, was like a dream come true. The nip in the air cleared our heads and invigorated our souls. Under the heavy cover of snow, the world was once again pristine and new, as if gifted with a new beginning.

But that was back then.

It's been twelve years now and not much has changed.

The snow refuses to melt and the sun only emits a flimsy, ghostly glow. Spring is a forgotten antiquity. As is autumn.

The locals yearn for the warmth of sunshine but no one quite remembers what summer used to be like.

Granny says she can send me back in time to return the winters and look for good summers.

But I resist.

I will have to let winter linger a wee bit longer. For I can't quite remember where in time each of the snowy patches ought to be sent back to.

∽

53

WHEN DRAGONS FORGET THEY CAN FLY

We asked the dragon what she was doing behind the fence.

She was waiting, she said. Waiting to be transported to her next destination.

Couldn't she simply fly, we asked.

No, she didn't think so. Well, she hadn't flown in a very long time, so she couldn't quite remember how to go about it anymore, she said.

No one can forget how to fly, we insisted. Just as people didn't forget how to walk or swim or ride a bike, even if they hadn't done it for decades.

That's not how it goes with flying, the dragon reasoned.

We couldn't argue for none of us had ever flown before nor did we know anyone else who could fly. (Except the birds, but they have long stopped sharing their secrets with humans, so there was no way we could verify the dragon's claims.)

We urged the dragon to try and fly.

Nah, she dismissed. It probably involved too much effort,

so she couldn't bothered to try, she said, and anyway she was scheduled to be transported to her next destination, the events crew should be here anytime now.

She said they'd dismantle her into small blocks, box them up, and piece her together again when they'd arrive at the next destination.

Didn't it hurt, we wondered.

It does, she admitted, but at least this way she knew she'd soon be whole and in one piece again. As long as she avoided the hazards of flying.

54

THE SEEING EYES

The eyes, they glow in the dark.

They watch, even if only in turns.

One keeps an eye (pun unintended) on your past to prevent it from slowing you down.

Another keeps watch on your future, ensuring it remains unknown and unpredictable enough to make life and its living interesting for you.

(No one watches your present, that responsibility is solely yours.)

The third monitors your friends, and the fourth, your enemies. Too many of one and too few of the other throws life out of balance.

The fifth eye keeps track of your luck, making sure you have enough when you need it the most, and that others get their fair share too.

The sixth eye watches from behind a closed lid. Every move, every breath, every thought and every hope, every heartbreak, every moment crushed under the weight of despair, every laughter that filled you with an indescribable lightness of being, the sixth eye records and remembers.

It flicks open only at the very end to help you remember an entire lifetime in a matter of moments.

One last time, a final memory, before your past and future, your friends and enemies, your good luck and bad, all cease to exist.

55

———

THE LETTER BOX

*I*t is our secret hiding place, where we leave things and stuff for each other.

At first we looked for a hollow in a tree, but most were already in use, crammed with other peoples' secrets.

So we decided to exchange our secrets in plain sight, in a letter box.

Mostly we leave letters for each other, sometimes written in code or using symbols, just to build an air of mystery for prying eyes, but usually stating nothing more than our love for each other.

When we are unable to write, we leave snippets of conversations. Words mingled with lilting voices and whispers.

Occasionally we leave songs, or poetry, or an oft repeated refrain, or other plays of words and music and melodies.

Sometimes we leave each other our thoughts, and that is how we find we can read each others' minds.

Sometimes he leaves me a rose, and I am enveloped in its fragrance all day.

I leave him a feather and his imagination takes flight.
That's how it works each time.
One from him, one from me.
Once he left me a life, and I used it to cheat Death.
I have yet to figure out what to give him in turn.

56

PAINTING THE POTS

The pots and vases stand bare and nude, having just emerged from the potter's wheel.

Each one is different from the other.

Each is unique.

But you can choose only one each year.

If you choose a pot that doesn't like you, you will have to give it up and wait an entire year before you can choose another.

Curved and moulded and shaped by the potter's hands, they stand tall and firm, and wait to be coloured and painted upon.

Some are painted in the colour of sunsets, the reds and yellows and oranges merging and fusing in a jovial dance.

Some are painted in the colour of peacock feathers, blues and purples and greens twirl and converge and diverge in little rivulets of colours.

A few are painted in monochrome, several others in motifs and designs painstakingly repeated with near-precision all over the surface.

Some are painted into invisibility.

Several others are painted into life, and they have minds of their own. They walk into houses they like and out of places they don't.

Every year people flock to the potter's to select their pots. Some opt for the large ones, others are content with smaller pieces that are just as exquisite. Some are drawn to the bright coloured ones, some others rub the rims of the pots to see if any have magical wish-granting traits.

But no one thinks to look inside.

None of the pots are painted on the inside.

Each bears a gift within.

Some carry the gift of happiness, some carry the gift of life.

A few (I can't quite remember exactly how many) bear youth, and only one holds immortality.

But you can pick only one pot each year.

They say immortality resides in the prettiest abodes, but I can't quite be certain of that.

57

THE STREET OF THE DEAD

The street is thronged with dead beings.

Zombies, vampires, ghouls, they rule this place.

Like monsters running amok on Halloween, the place is littered with all kinds of dead beings — the half-deads, the ones barely alive, some who died barely a moment ago and are only getting used to the sudden turn of events in their lives and deaths, and then those who died several deaths every day, and then some more.

Every evening they emerge on to the street, dressed in their finest, from the edges of existence. They wriggle out from the cracks in tombstones. They bleed into existence from the horizon. They surface from the walls that partition homes.

The vampires sashay in their overrated capes, hissing and flashing their fangs at innocent bystanders. Some of the dead are reduced to bare-bones, their dead, decaying skin clinging to their skeletal frames. Some others, freshly lowered into their graves, appear rosy-cheeked and wide-eyed.

There are no leaders, no followers. There are only those who have walked the street a countless times, and those who are new to the ways of this world.

Every evening they stomp down the street in revelry, sharing stories of their past lives, and their hopes and dreams for future ones.

Some look forward to their new lives, others are unhappy to have lost their old ones.

Sooner or later, however, they make their peace and step off the street, back into the world of the living.

Truth be told, even on the street they are more alive than dead.

58

WELL-INTENTIONED ADVICE FOR CHILDREN LEFT UNATTENDED TO

Children unattended to will be given espresso and a free kitten.

As you sip your coffee and help yourself to some cookies, your child can choose from among pixie-bobs, ragamuffins, ragdolls, ocicats, Persian kittens, munchkins, minskins, Australian Mists, and Abyssinian cats.

Whichever your little one chooses, the kitten will wrap itself around your child's legs and cast a benign, binding spell.

The kitten will then lead your little girl or boy to the park across the road.

(Oh, don't bother to look. The park is not visible to adults. Only little children and kittens can see it.)

The park has a jungle gym to climb on to, rabbit holes to fall into, stars to count all night, and invisible friends to talk to.

When your child has had their fill of the park, the kitten will lead your little one through the hedgerows to the other side where treasure-hunters are digging a hole through the earth to someplace yet to be discovered.

We hear the hunters have very nearly completed digging the hole, so your child could be the lucky first to disappear through it and reappear in a new land, halfway across the world on the other side.

(Oh, don't you worry, dear parents. Your children will be completely safe with the kittens by their side. And if you insist, they can always come back from the new land in a jiffy simply by sailing over the rainbow.)

If the hole has not been completely dug, the kitten will lead your child beyond to meet The Famous Five. The Five — (and Timothy the dog will be there too!) — are a jolly bunch and they will welcome your child to join them on their summertime camping adventures.

When the summer holidays are over and the Five have to return home, the kitten will lead your child to the wise man's hut, where he has a stash of fairy tales to regale them with. He will read stories to your child until the little one falls asleep, and the kitten will then bring your young one back to you.

You must then take your child home, tuck them in, kiss them goodnight, and leave them to dream of fairylands and magic and adventures.

The only trouble is, when your child wakes up the next morning, they will go looking for the adventures they dreamt about. Nothing you say or do will dissuade them.

So, dear parents, if you don't want your children to go seeking adventures you think do not exist, please do not leave them unattended to.

59

A BIRTHDAY WISH

I want to be
the crest of the wave that crashes on the shore
and sweeps away all the seashells on its way out,

the poetry that rides on the flutter of the breeze until the
muse traps it on paper,

the music that emanates from a hollow, broken piece of
wood held together by strings,

the melody that yields a new hidden note each time you
replay it on the tape,

the quiver in the singer's voice as she lets a note linger a
tad longer than you can hold your breath,

the story you want to read over and over again until you
have committed each exquisite word, each beautiful turn of
phrase to memory,

the colours that bleed from the artist's brush on to the
canvas, rich and resplendent at first, but fading away with
the passage of time,

the drop of water that glides down a wet lock of hair and
hangs like a teardrop at the end,

the memory that has lodged itself so deep into the recesses of your mind that you know it exists, but the more you try to retrieve it, the farther out of reach it slips,

the heartbreak that sits at the base of your throat like a lump that won't go away, no matter how many tears you shed,

the hollow in your gut that your sorrow carves out, inch by hurting inch, as you realize your loss is irreconcilable,

the slow, steady movement of the second hand that stretches your wait to eternity,

the faint flicker of hope that tries to warm your lonely heart on a cold winter's day,

your thoughts, your memories, your hopes, your fears, your desires, your dreams,

everything that makes your heart beat, that makes the blood course through your veins faster and furiouser.

I want to be everything that makes you come alive.

60

REINDEER ON STRIKE

All the reindeer had gone on strike.

And so Santa had resorted to travelling in a time-and-space capsule.

"Modern times! Need to keep up with technology, eh," he retorted when we asked him about the missing reindeer.

The reindeer, he said, are protesting long working hours and demanding higher wages. And since nothing could be done about their complaints, they had decided to freeze in time, Santa said. The "stubborn creatures" (his words, not ours) had become useless when it came to drawing sleighs.

"Lazy creatures with their brains caught in their antlers," he snorted as he heaved himself down our chimney.

A sack of presents came tumbling down after him.

He brushed the soot off his garments, his chirpily red coat and trousers laced with sparkling white cuffs, not a speck of dust or soot from the chimney on them nor on his snowy white hair and beard.

"The capsule is not all that bad," he continued, as he proceeded to stack our presents under the Christmas tree.

"It's incredibly fast. I can go anywhere in the blink of an eye," he said, stressing he needs the speed in order to cater to six billion gift-seekers in a single night.

"What about tradition?" we asked. "The stories don't talk about time capsules, the carols we sing are about reindeer and sleighs," we insisted.

"That was then, this is now," he brushed us off. He then emerged from under the tree, warned us to be good children and not go peeking into the gifts before morning, and wished us all a merry Christmas, before scampering up the chimney and out of sight.

The next morning we opened our presents to find nine little reindeer figurines, one with a bright red nose. There was also a note from Santa, asking us to look after the nine reindeer. "Keep them by the fireside, and they will unfreeze with time," he instructed us.

It's been almost a year now.

Last month, we moved the reindeer closer to the fireside.

Last week, they started to stir.

One went missing this morning.

We think the rest should be back in action before time.

61

FLOWERS FOR WHEN HE'S GONE

The flowers arrive unexpectedly.

They weren't suppose to arrive until Valentine's.

But here they are now, all these months ahead of time.

Which means I will not see him until after then.

A little knot of fear rises from the pit of my stomach, lodges itself firmly in my head, and causes my heart to flap.

I run a finger over the petals. They shiver under my touch.

I look for a note in the bouquet. There is none.

I place the flowers in water, and let them be.

It's been a week now.

The roses are still in full bloom, the petals soft and tender.

Now it's been a month and I have seen the roses turn different shades of red.

Sometimes they are the vermillion streaks of sunset, at other times they take on the colour of blood.

When the mood strikes, they dazzle brilliantly like rubies.

173

Sometimes the phone rings and he tells me he is headed to distant lands, at other times I can say he's been hurt even if he doesn't always confide.

There are times when he finds the answers he is seeking, and I wish he'd finally make his way home. But then I can also tell he is dreaming of other adventures to pursue, mysteries to unravel.

It has taken me a while to decipher the code but the flowers are my constant companions now. I can discern the slightest shift in colour, the faintest alteration in tint, all in just a momentary glance. And I'd know if he is safe or happy or in danger or sad even if he doesn't always tell.

He hasn't called in a while now.

The roses have mostly been a dazzling crimson these past few days, so alive, so bright I think there is mescaline coursing through my veins.

A glint here, a sparkle there.

Like a candle sputtering and shimmering right before the end.

And now they have burst into flames.

And before I can do anything, a little ball of fire collapses into itself and vanishes from sight.

I stand looking, staring at vacant space, not quite knowing what to make of it all, when the doorbell rings.

~

62

BIRDS OF A FEATHER FLOCK
TOGETHER

Folklore has it that long, long ago, all living beings spoke the same language.

(Of course, this was all long before mankind and animals and birds went their separate ways and conjured up their own secret tongues so as to keep from each other what they really thought about the other and what they planned to inflict upon each other.)

But back when everyone understood each other, and the world was in peace and harmony, it was the ravens that were mankind's trusted messengers. Not the pigeons. The use of pigeons to ferry messages across mountains and seas was a romantic notion that took root much later.

The bearer of messages has a very important role to play.

His is a task that requires much wit, deep awareness, the ability to make complex decisions in the face of danger, bravery so as to not allow any private messages to be intercepted, and enough empathy so as to be able to express joy when the message is a happy one and convey dignified solemnity when the news to be conveyed in tragic.

175

These were the qualities in ravens that made them aptly suitable for the job.

Above all, what set the ravens apart from other living beings was the speed and efficiency they exhibited in transmitting messages, thanks to their knowledge of the shortest routes and paths, which enabled them to travel as the crow flies.

Of course it helped that the ravens were found in abundance — in the jungles, on the streets, on treetops, in people's backyards, in their gardens, on their windowsills eating breadcrumbs, and sometimes inside their kitchens if no one was looking.

Our big, black birds found it offensive to have rolls of paper tethered to their claws. They preferred, instead, to have the addressor tell them the message, which they were then happy to repeat to the recipient.

As I said, this was back in the times when all living beings spoke the same tongue. So this did not pose any problem at first, and the message creators and receivers were only too happy with this arrangement, as were the ravens who were politely treated to goodies every time they received or imparted a message.

All the trouble started when the ravens started to contort the messages. At first it was harmless distortion, and some of the misrepresentations were in fact very funny to begin with, created out of boredom and the overall monotonous nature of their work and lives.

But then the ravens took to telling tales and lies, and in no time untruths and falsifications were being transmitted back and forth until eventually mankind declared war on the animals over a simple misunderstanding and the world was engulfed in several decades of violence and mayhem.

Did you know?

One of the collective nouns for a group of ravens is a *storytelling* of ravens.

At another period of time, when pigeons began to rise to the fore as messengers of love, the ravens took to stealing the pigeons' eggs out of spite. They, the ravens, reckoned that if they could stymie the growth in pigeon population, the ravens would regain what they considered their rightful place as trustworthy and reliable messengers of the living world.

It did not take long for the rest of the world to figure out what the ravens were up to, which only made pigeons more popular than before.

Did you know?

One of the collective nouns for a group of ravens is an *unkindness* of ravens.

Before long, mankind learned not to trust anybody but his own clan and started to deliver messages by hand.

Did you know?

One of the collective nouns for a group of ravens is a *nevermore* of ravens.

Enraged by the 'disrespect' they perceived, the ravens took to ambushing human messengers whenever the latter had to travel through thick jungles and forests. Clad in shockingly black feathers, the ravens were indiscernible from the thick blackness of the night, so no one could ever tell who was responsible for the attacks.

Did you know?

One of the collective nouns for a group of ravens is a *conspiracy* of ravens.

So as to not lose any more of his brothers and sisters, mankind developed advanced technologies that would obey his command and do no more or no less than instructed to. This involved the erection of transmission poles and wires to dispatch messages in the form of invisible little pieces of information strung together by invisible threads of ... well, invisible stuff.

The ravens, helpless when confronted with things they had little clue about, then took to sitting on telephone wires yelling blue murder, crowing and cawing about the unfairness of it all, but with little action to back up their claims.

Everyone ignores them, and now no one understands anymore what the ravens cry about, perched above the world and dumping turd on unsuspecting passersby.

Did you know?

One of the collective nouns for a group of ravens is a *parliament* of ravens.

63

———

MAKING NEW ROADS

$\mathcal{I}$t is difficult to track down the road-maker.

Word has it that there is very little that gives away his presence, especially when he is at work.

He works quietly and swiftly, and you know he's been there only after he is long gone, leaving behind a trail of new roads where none existed before, perhaps to make up for the old roads that disappeared as if the earth had swallowed them up in the dead of the night.

It was the end of the year 2012, and the world had not met its end, so some of us resuscitated long-forgotten dreams. And now we wanted to seek out the road-maker so he could build us new paths to traverse in the new year.

Someone said they had spotted him at the town's inn the evening before, enjoying a drink and making merry. We hurried towards the inn but, as we had half-expected, the inn was closed and we learnt that the innkeeper had set out to travel the world, following new paths no doubt laid by the road-maker.

Someone else said the road-maker was last seen by the

edge of the river, erecting a bridge across the waters to the city. We rushed to the river bank only to see a newly-laid bridge disappearing before our very eyes, and a glimpse of the road-maker disappearing into the city lights yonder.

Our search for the road-maker was fruitless, nevertheless we decided to plod on towards the city following well-trodden paths. This was in early 2013.

And looking back now, we can safely say it has turned out to be a year of adventures and discoveries. We stuck to established paths at first, then allowed ourselves to meander a bit and stumbled upon hidden routes; the more adventurous among us blazed new trails, some of us ran into dead ends and had to retrace our steps and start all over again.

The funny part was that in all this we had forgotten all about the road-maker. So when he approached our table at the newest pub in the city, where we had gathered for an evening of celebration on the last day of 2013, and greeted us, we were more than a bit startled.

He apologized for the delay but stressed his was not to simply unfurl new paths at our feet when we stood still. His was to help keep the momentum going.

And that is how when dawn broke over the new year this time, we found ourselves on new paths paved by the road-maker. And we found he had also thrown in a few new dreams for good measure.

∼

64

THE TALKING SKULL

It begins with a low rumbling noise.

The sound of something far away.

Like thunder in the distance.

Or water tumbling off the vertical slopes of a cliff.

Rolling towards me urgently, surging in intensity.

And if I listen keenly for a while, tuning out the rest of the world, I can begin to discern the chuckles and the words and then the sentences and what they mean.

And I wonder from where all the words of wisdom are being hurled at me.

And I look around to see the the grinning skull talking to me.

His grin is evil, his laughter hideous, his eyes hollow with bottomless depths, but there is a sincerity in his words, which makes it hard for me to ignore him and walk away.

The post-it stuck to his forehead says mysteriously, 'Take a penny, Leave a penny.'

I deposit a coin in front of the skull, and he tells me a life secret.

181

I fish for another coin in my purse and place it by his chin.

He shares another life secret.

He is eager for more pennies, and I for words of wisdom, and that makes him garrulous.

When I run out of pennies, he says he can trade his secrets for mine.

The rule, however, is to take only as much as I can leave behind for him.

Momma says the talking skull is an absolute liar and that I shouldn't trust him with my secrets.

So I am thinking maybe I could trade in my stories instead.

I hope he will like them enough.

65

THE GYPSY WITH MAGIC IN
HER EYES

She is a gypsy, a wandering wild soul who has a camera for a second eye.

Oh yes, she can read you your fortune and tell you all that lies ahead. Not necessarily the truth, but that depends on how much you are willing to pay her, as is the case with most gypsies.

But she is special.

One fleeting glimpse at you through her little thingamajig, and your darkest fears and most shimmering dreams reveal themselves to her like sunbeams surfing on ocean waves.

You halt for an instant, she captures a moment of you in time, and your future unfurls itself at her feet.

If she likes your expression in the snapshot, she will, if you'd like her to, make a cut here, a snip there, and alter your fate to your liking. That is her idea of fun and mischief for she is a princess of the wild.

If you let her look into your eyes for far too long, she will pluck out your soul, infuse it with some magic, and press it back into you. And she does all this in a very practiced sleight of hand, so you will wake up the next morning not knowing why your entire being appears to be so imbued with hope and optimism.

Sometimes she does things without being asked to.

If she thinks you will put your time on earth to good use, she will stretch your future a wee bit further than was granted to you.

If she is convinced otherwise, there is no telling what she might do.

But that is a risk you must be willing to take if you want her to meddle with your future.

66

THE TWO WORLDS AND THE FENCE
IN BETWEEN

A thin fence separates the two worlds.

It isn't clear which world stakes a claim to the fence itself.

Perhaps it is the other world — some of their folk seem to be always sitting on the fence.

Sometimes one of them falls over to our side. He then quickly springs up, mutters an apology, dusts himself, and jumps back on to the fence or over it and saunters away on the other side.

Most of us in our world want to be neither on the fence nor on the other side. We are happy where we are and, if given a choice, would like to stay here forever.

But sometimes one of our own tries to blend in with the other-worldly folk.

Sometimes they pass on.

More commonly, they tread precariously on the fence, as if attempting a delicate tightrope walk between this world and the other.

Sometimes they fall back on to our side.

Sometimes the other side wins. But only if their time has come.

Of course, none of us gets to choose when the time is right.

~

67

THE LITTLE DOOR AND THE PIXIE
WHO LIVES BEHIND IT

They say a little pixie lives in the tiny house at the base of the largest magnolia tree in the village.

No one has seen her though, so you could argue the house belongs to a pixie or an elf or a dwarf or even to you, and you wouldn't be wrong.

But someone does live there, they say.

A little someone who keeps the fire roaring in the little fireplace in her little home so that weary passersby on a black night are guided by the light, and the homeless and the abandoned can huddle around her tree for warmth.

A little someone who climbs up to the highest points of the tree before the break of dawn and quietly jiggles the branches, so when the village begins to stir and people look out their windows towards the new day, they see lush carpets of delicate pink flowers on their streets and smile to themselves, thinking what a beautiful world we all live in.

If she likes you, she will sometimes rustle the leaves and shower you with flowers as you walk under her tree.

A little someone who leaves cute little things in the

hollow of her tree for inquisitive children to find. Sometimes the good children leave behind little things for their invisible friend too — a marble of the colour of the deepest oceans and the bluest skies, a spinning top that goes round and round the magnolia tree until you command it to stop, sometimes a balloon that the pixie could hold on to and fly away over the treetops into the mountains beyond — magic-ky little things that she loves.

Some of the kids say they have visited the pixie at her home (and yes, she is a pixie, not an elf nor a dwarf, they say).

We call their bluff and say they are too big to wriggle through the little door.

They say they nibble on the mushrooms that grow outside her door, and they shrink enough to be able to enter.

And — they add before we can contest — on the way out, they nibble on another mushroom and grow back to their full size.

Well, children have such active imaginations we simply cannot fault them for spinning such lovely tales.

So when they pluck a mushroom from her doorstep and hand it out to us, we thank them and politely take a few bites.

Of course, there are no such things as pixies and magic mushrooms in real life, we tell ourselves.

But I secretly hope we turn out to be wrong.

68

THE STAIRWAY TO A SECRET PLACE

*O*nly a few people can see it, but if you look hard enough you most certainly will spot the stairway.

It rises from the roots of an ancient tree, runs around its trunk, and disappears from view around the corner. The only way to tell where it leads to is to traverse it.

If you were to ask the townspeople about it, they would unanimously tell you that it leads to a secret place. But each one has a different definition for his or her secret place.

For one, it is a haven from the mundane dreariness of the real world.

For another, it is a place where fairytales come true.

Yet another believes it is a place where they can safely hide from their demons, while a fourth would consider it a safe spot to indulge in their deepest, darkest fantasies without any fear of retribution.

I think that all these people, the ones who sit under the stars and contemplate the secret place, make up these stories and ideas in their wandering minds, often with little clue as to what they are talking about.

For, the ones who have gone and truly explored the stairway have not yet returned from their secret place or wherever the stairs led them to.

But those were the brave souls, the ones that ventured, I can now say.

I have lost count of how many steps I have climbed so far. I can neither remember the beginning, nor see how and where my journey will end.

But this much I know. The townspeople think the first step is always the hardest. But that is far from the truth.

The first step is perhaps among the easiest. It is harder to keep going when you fear you are lost.

69

THE BABY SHOE

The baby shoe lay on the pavement like a forgotten promise.

It betrayed no clues as to who and where its wearer was.

Some worried a little child may have gone missing. Abandoned, but with a pink shimmer of hope, as if it were waiting for a rescue it knew would never come.

The notion sent a collective sigh of pathos among the crowd.

Some others harboured less sinister thoughts and believed the shoe may have fallen from a baby's dangling leg or out of an overflowing shopping-bag.

Some thought the child may have fallen into the sewer, or better still, leapt into it out of curiosity, one shoe left behind.

Somebody wistfully said the child may have grown up too quickly and so the shoe no longer fit.

Somebody else then asked where the other shoe was.

Truth was, it was just another *baby shoe, never worn, for sale*, having fallen off the truck en route from the factory of mass production to the retail shop of luxury; but no one wanted to believe something so devoid of emotion.

70

THE THREE WISE MEN BY THE WINDOW SILL

The three wise men hang around by the window sill all day long and dole out prophecies to innocent passersby.

Trouble is, no one can hear them. Even if they do, the passersby just pretend that the voices coming out of nowhere are only figments of their imagination.

But that does not stop the three wise men from sharing their wisdom with the world.

They now resort to shining brightly to grab the attention of the accidental receivers of wisdom.

The wise man on the left starts to shimmer and glitter if he knows your past is about to catch up with you. The past may well be long gone, but nothing stops it from shaping your present and your future, he believes.

The one on the right glistens and glimmers to let you know a glorious destiny awaits you, whatever your past may have been. Obviously, he is always at loggerheads with the one on the left, and both try to outdo the other in guiding the passersby. Today he shines so brightly you are blinded by the promises of what the future might bring; so you forget your past and trip over today in reckless haste.

The wise man in the middle rarely shines. People rarely notice him, so he ignores them too.

He shakes his head at his quarrelling partners.

"Fools," he laughs.

We know not whether he is ridiculing his partners or his mockery is aimed at you, you who is running away from your past and hurtling impatiently into the future.

71

IN SEARCH OF PARADISE

I learnt from the townsfolk that all the Gods and most of the angels have taken to hiding, now that human beings no longer believe in Paradise.

But, they add, if I were to persist in my search, I could find an angel or two lurking about near the cave hidden behind the waterfall at the end of the world.

The thought that angels could still be found at the end of the world was both poignant and amusing at the same time, and I tell them so, but the townsfolk only stare at me in uncomprehending silence.

I was never good at making jokes anyway, I say, both for my benefit and theirs, and before anyone can respond I heave my rucksack further up my back and make my way to the cave.

True enough, I spot a couple of angels at the entrance to the cave but there are no other human beings in sight, so I believe this is the end of the world, at least as I know it.

I ask the angels if I have indeed reached the end of the world.

"It depends," the younger one replies, "on whether you want to halt here or proceed further."

"What lies beyond?" I ask.

"Paradise, perhaps?" the younger one teases and giggles.

The older angel shushes her and turns to me, "No one can definitely say what lies beyond. Sometimes the celestial beings know, but we are forbidden from sharing our knowledge with you. It is for you to venture and find out."

I rarely turn down an offer for an adventure, so I bid the angels farewell and step over the edge. I fall for what could have been eternity or merely a fraction of a second, and when I land on my feet, I find myself in a new world.

A world of unfamiliar faces and unknown languages, of new stories and age-old folklore. A world where I am stripped of all knowledge of the past, a life that stretches ahead of me like a blank slate on which I must piece a new story together.

It takes me a lifetime to learn and adapt to the ways of the new world, even though I can never master it. When I feel I have had my fill, I set out, once again, on my journey to the end of this world.

And again I meet the two angels, the young one and the old one, and they make me the same offer yet again. Call it a day or explore a new world in the hope it would turn out to be my Paradise.

I have lost count of the number of worlds I have traversed thus far. But what really worries me is the nagging doubt that I may have crossed Paradise long back and not even realized it.

~

72

IT'S SHOWTIME!

*C*ome, come, my dearies!
     Hurry up!
You need to get dressed for the show, the stage is all set, and there isn't much time left.

Grab your costumes, and put on your make-up.

Scarlet lipsticks, and midnight mascaras.

Violet eyes, and shiny noses.

Brush the rouge on your cheeks, dab some perfume on your wrists, so you smell like oriental lilies and shimmer like the stars.

Rehearse your lines.

But if you forget them while on stage, fear not.

Tell a tale, whistle a tune, or break into a song.

Just don't let the silence linger on for too long.

We've been here countless times before.

We will do this umpteen times again.

You only get better each time.

So worry not, if you make new mistakes.

Remember, everything is acceptable, as long as you remain true to your character.

73

THE TRAIL

We are quite a noisy bunch but we manage to remain out of sight.

The travellers journeying across the path mistake us for the rustle of leaves or for invisible creatures slithering through the undergrowth, shying away from humans.

Which suits us well enough.

We do not seek to make ourselves known, at least not to everybody.

We merely want to get close enough to the path to eavesdrop on the wanderers without revealing our presence.

Most travellers stick to the path, occasionally pausing to catch their breath, peer into the woods, and wonder what lies beyond. Mostly, they choose not to satisfy their curiosity, and after a brief pause, they continue onwards.

Some think a paradise of sorts awaits them at the end of the path, what with the town council — in its schemes to lure more tourists to the forgotten region — having advertised breathtaking views overlooking cliffs and oceans to be found at the end of the trail.

Some others believe the journey is more significant than the destination, and seek to enjoy the pleasures of walking down the trail, one hidden turn leading to another.

Often they try to capture the sights and sounds and smells in their cameras, creating a heap of pictures that never receive a second glance; they are forgotten no sooner than they are clicked.

We usually wait for the lone travellers who seek us out and talk to us.

We do not see them as often as we would like but when they do come, we delight in their visits and the intelligent conversations they make.

They inquire after the creatures of the land, and ask us questions about the trail and its history.

How old is the trail?

Older than the sun and the moon.

Who created the trail?

The creatures that live in the woods.

Where are those creatures now?

They are labelled extinct but in truth they remain cleverly hidden in the woods.

Sometimes they ask us tricky questions.

Once a little girl asked if the trail leads to heaven.

No, it does not, no matter what your idea of heaven may be, we answered.

Then how do I get to heaven, she asked.

But we didn't know what to say. We do not always have appropriate answers to their questions.

~

74

A PROMISING CAREER AS A PIRATE

The pirates are recruiting.

They are looking for story-tellers, magicians, flame-throwers, illusionists, rainbow-makers, dream-weavers, mermaid-spotters and the like who can regale and entertain the pirates when they settle down amid their treasure chests guzzling bottles of rum after a long hard day at work.

Applications are invited from anyone who can take figments of their imagination and convert them into reality.

Prior expertise is not a requirement but candidates must exhibit a keen desire to learn and perform; the best candidates are usually the ones who are not embarrassed to make mistakes and be mocked at.

Interested candidates are to address their applications to the pirates' ship, Moonbeam Warrior, and successfully complete a series of tasks before they are called for an interview.

(Finding where the ship is located is the first task.)

Your remuneration will comprise half a treasure map,

bottles of rum, coins of gold and silver (sometimes these may be fake as a testimony to your performance or lack of it), more bottles of rum, cigars, and the luxury of nights spent under the stars ; there is no such thing as health insurance, and God forbid, should you fall seasick, you will be tossed overboard without a second thought, so consider yourself warned.

The more creative your application, the better your chances at being recruited, but the pirates are obviously not equal-opportunity employers; the best job always goes to the one who supplies them with an endless stash of rum.

The deadline for applications was a century ago, but as with every other rule, this too can be bent with a crate or two full of their liquor of choice.

(Psst! Moonbeam Warrior, docked at the harbour, is hidden in plain sight; but busy drivers on the adjacent highway easily mistake her proud, rusty masts for worn-out streetlight poles.)

75

THE SECRET WORK OF ROAD-PAINTERS TOILING IN THE NIGHT-TIME

The road-painters work together in large numbers, swiftly but quietly.

They work only at night, always by the silver light of the shape-shifting moon.

The colours they use come from various sources; green from the leaves, crimson from the setting sun, indigo from the rainbow, lilac from the rhododendrons, and very often they mix up the colours to create new ones that have not yet been named.

The colours are always stolen but the road-painters insist it is not so much *'stealing'* as it is *'borrowing'* because the signs they paint always lead the travellers back to where the colours originally came from. And, the road-painters argue, they keep none of the colours for themselves but use all of their loot instead for the greater good.

Tonight the road-painters are painting blue leaves on the hard concrete; they have taken some of the blue from the skies and some from the ocean depths and have mixed the two together to create a new sort of an in-between but a familiar I-have-seen-it-before kind of blue.

Tomorrow the skies and the sea waves will look rather grey, having lost some of their blueness to the road-painters.

But travellers chasing the blue leaves painted overnight will find that the path eventually leads them to their own perfect piece of blue sky or a dreamy ocean, or whatever their idea of blue paradise may have been.

The road-painters like to think of themselves as modern-day Robin Hood and his Merry Men, stealing from the riches of nature to lure wanderers and lost travellers back to nature's lap.

But the road-painters never steal the silver of the light-pilfering moon. It is an unwritten code of honour among thieves, they do not steal from each other.

76

THE TOWER OF THE GUARDIANS OF THE WORLD

Grandma said the tower was built by the Guardians of the World so that they could climb atop it and keep an eye on any danger seen heading towards our world.

But that does not make sense, I cried, because I could see that the tower is not very tall and is very easily dwarfed by the maple trees that surround it in the park.

Grandma looked up, put her hand above her eyes as if to shield them from the setting sun, and tut-tutted that that top of the tower was nowhere to be seen.

I pointed to the top and said it was right there, and how could she not see it, maybe her eyes were playing tricks on her, because the top of the tower was as visible as clear daylight.

She turned to me, her blue-grey eyes naughtily twinkling with secrets and mischief, and I worried that she may not have believed my claims.

So before she could say anything, I told her I would scale up and down the tower in less than a quarter of an hour, it really wasn't that tall, to which she replied that I could very well proceed with my monkey tricks and that she was only happy to wait for me for she had all the time in the world to spare and that she was in no hurry to be anywhere else.

It was an easy climb; the tower offered several footholds and cracks and crevices, all in the right places and just large enough for me to push my ten-year-old feet into.

I climbed, higher and higher, and very soon I could see over the tops of the trees and view the meadows that lay beyond, and I climbed some more until I could see the clouds coming to kiss my feet, and then some more from where I could see as far as the edge of the world and the sun slowly slipping behind it, and I kept going until it grew dark and there were stars in the night sky above me and below me and all around me.

But I couldn't find the top of the tower, and seeing the black sky all around me I started to feel a wee bit scared, and my thoughts turned to Grandma who was perhaps all alone in the dark park now and I worried about her and started to climb down.

On the way down, I crossed the silver stars in the black sky, and then white clouds in a purple sky, and then there was the red sun still reluctant to slip behind the edge of the world, and at last I could see the top of the maple trees and finally the top of Grandma's head, and when my feet finally landed on the ground I ran to her and hugged her and excitedly described to her all the things I saw, and I could tell that this time she believed every single word of it.

～

77

A DEAL WITH THE DEVIL

I had been trying to summon an angel but Satan showed up instead.

He did not look particularly frightening; he looked like he had been painted near-black from head to toe with occasional splotches of verdigris and sienna, as if parts of him were peeling away to reveal a more colourful self hidden underneath.

I tried to shoo him away but he refused to leave the pavilion where he had popped up.

"You summoned me," he stated the obvious. "I cannot leave unless I grant you a wish."

His voice was deep and smooth, rumbling up from the bottomless depths of his netherworld and rising up to his throat like a wicked yet sad laughter, both dangerous and poignant all at once.

I knew better than to make a deal with the devil, we all know how badly such things end, and so, touched by his generosity although I was, I nonetheless declined his offer politely.

"No, you do not understand," he stood his ground. "You summoned me. I am bound to you unless I grant you a wish. It is the rule of such things. I cannot leave until I have fulfilled what I was sent for."

"Isn't is true that devils cannot grant wishes without taking away a part of the wish-seeker's soul?" I asked.

He hung his head sadly and gave a slight nod. "But I used to be an angel once, you know. A very, very long time ago. I am not sure if that counts for anything at all."

I could not think of a suitable response.

"They used to call me Lucifer back then," he continued, his gaze abstractedly fixed on something beyond the edges of the planet. "It means the morning star."

I made my wish then, and asked him to send me back in time so I could seek out Lucifer and summon him before he falls.

78

THE MUSIC OF ANGELS AT UNGODLY HOURS

The angels play their most beautiful music at in-between times.

Sometimes they bring out their horns between midnight and the thirteenth hour.

Sometimes their music fills the skies in the moments between yesterday and today.

They do not follow a schedule.

But it is said that they play their best melodies just after the blackness of the night sky begins to fade and turns into cobalt blue but just before the songbirds commence their dawn chorus.

Their music floats into the aether at moments when one thing ends and gives way to the beginning of something new.

When transitory, life-altering moments slice the grand concept of your lifetime into before and after periods.

Not everyone can hear the music though.

It is a privilege reserved only for the newborns and the dying.

At the beginning of a new life or when an old one nears its end.

I suppose that is when we feel the most alive.

79

ESSENTIAL INSTRUCTIONS FOR WEAVING A MAGIC CARPET AND USING IT WELL

1 **Choosing your Colours**

First you must choose your yarns.

There are many, many colours to choose from.

Most customers make the mistake of choosing very few colours or only their favourite colours, which they soon outgrow.

It is advisable to choose plenty of your favourites but also just as many as the ones you're not particularly fond of. Choosing too many of one kind over the other will render the carpet unbalanced.

If none of the colours on display bear distinct appeal to your finer taste, we recommend you mix two or more skeins and wait for the colours to transform into surprising new ones.

2 **Elements of Design**

Once you have chosen your colours, you will need to conjure up a design.

It is recommended that no two of your favourite colours are woven alongside each other, because when the carpet starts to unravel, you do not want all your favourite colours falling out and apart all at once.

(Please note, every carpet is guaranteed to unravel on several occasions in the course of its lifetime; there is no way to avoid such inevitabilities. The sole recourse on such occasions is to slowly put all the threads back together again; you could retrace the original design or create a new one.)

Carpet-weavers are advised to first create only an initial draft of their design and to NOT plan its intricacies in vivid detail for reasons that are elucidated in the section that follows.

3 **Weaving the Carpet**
When you start to weave, you will find that some, or many, yarns will simply not be woven according to your design.

They will resist and turn and twist in directions other than where you'd like them to go. Some yarns can be browbeaten into submission but this is not at all advisable.

Magical objects have minds of their own, and tampering with their wishes can yield consequences far more frightening than the human mind can conceive.

Our advice is to let the stubborn yarns weave and coil themselves into patterns as they please.

Happy yarns make a happy carpet.

And more often than not, customers have been delighted with the new patterns that their yarns conjure up for them.

. . .

4 Flying on the Carpet

Firstly, you must step on to the carpet gently.

No carpet likes to be trampled upon, so please exhibit utmost care and tenderness especially on your first mount.

Ensconce yourself in the centre.

When you are ready, run your fingers gently over the threads and tell the carpet where you would like to go.

When the carpet starts to tremble and quiver, and pretends as if it will knock you off, remember to sit back, relax, and enjoy the ride.

For all the magic carpet asks of you is to have a little faith in its abilities.

80

DANGERS IN THE WOODS

*D*on't be fooled! The scenery is breathtaking but these are the most dangerous parts of the woods.

Travellers would do well to stay in groups. (In fact, they would do well to stay away from the woods altogether.)

But if you must travel, you must seek refuge in numbers, and although that does not guarantee safety, a lone traveller will almost never make it alive to the other side.

You could consider donning invisibility cloaks for protection, but they are rare to find and obtain, and if you do wear one, there are things in the woods that even magic cannot protect you from.

The woods are lush and green, but invisible creatures prowl among the trees hunting for fresh souls to prey upon.

The water is cool as ice and fresh as dew, but underwater beasts lurk just below the surface, tempting you to dip your feet in the water, where they wait, ready to yank you into bottomless depths.

The bridge offers the only escape from the woods.

But when it grows dark, it vanishes from right under your feet.

Even if you are only halfway through it.

81

THE ELVES AND THE STORY-MAKER

Many a night have I sat hunched over my desk, filling reams of paper with inky words written in an elaborately cursive hand. And many a morning after have I spent discarding much of the prose and verses that had sprung to life the previous night.

So when the two elves knock at my window this fine night, I let them in and offer them tea and cookies. They sit by the fireplace, and at their insistence I half-heartedly read out some of my work to them in my best story-telling voice.

When I finish reading, they exchange thoughtful glances with each other and momentarily speak in a language I do not understand. The older of the two elves then turns to me and, with much more gravity than the situation warrants, says, "These are not half bad but we could help you improve."

I want to jump up and down in delight and readily accept their offer, but something reminds me that magic, both good and bad, always comes with a price, and so I ask the elves to name theirs.

The older elf is not pleased with my question but he

discloses, "Once we work through your stories, the words are cast in stone."

"Yes, you make them up, we make them real," the younger elf chimes in.

I thank them for their offer and politely say I need more time to think about it. After all, my stories are inspired by real life and my characters are based on real people, so this is not a decision I could take without giving it due thought.

I offer the elves more tea but they decline, saying they better be going, they have many more story-makers' homes to visit, but they promise to come back tomorrow night and say they hope I would have made up my mind by then about using their services.

As soon as they leave, I begin to make a list of all the characters I could plot to kill in my forthcoming stories.

82

WORDS OF WISDOM FROM THE WISE OLD MEN

The two old men sit next to each other in the showcase that adorns an entire wall in the living room of our home.

Mother brought them back from her travels to an otherworld last month.

"Looking at their amused faces reminds me to be happy," she said the day she gently peeled off the paper-wrapping from the velvet box they were ensconced in and placed them tenderly in the showcase.

I don't think she has given them a second glance since.

They are a funny pair.

All day long they crack jokes and entertain each other, and amuse me whenever I am within earshot.

They often joke about the members of our household. They laugh the most at the antics of Dover, our golden retriever, who tries to leap up and knock them down but they remain out of reach and he goes back to scowling at them from under the sofa.

They are mostly nice to me, sharing their jokes and

making me laugh, and sometimes they make fun of me and I end up laughing at myself.

When I recount their conversations to Mother, she says figurines cannot talk.

And I insist that they do, at least these two do.

At first Mother does not argue, but after a few occasions she knits her eyebrows and says she is beginning to worry about me.

And I tell her that she has no cause for worry, especially not if I am happy.

She considers that thought for several moments and finally cautions me to not have make-believe conversations with the figurines anymore; after all I am too old to have imaginary friends, she says.

"Not even if it makes me happy?" I ask.

No, comes the stern reply.

And so I promise her, my fingers crossed behind my back.

When Mother leaves the room, the two old men tell me not to worry about the things she said.

"No harm ever came from being happy," they assure me.

83

THE CLANDESTINE MEETING OF GODS TO DISCUSS THE GROWING WISH-LISTS OF HUMAN BEINGS

The Gods come from afar, and one by one they plant themselves on the wall.

The ones that arrived first have chosen the best spots they could find, but more and more Gods are on their way and there is growing concern there may not be adequate room for all.

Such a congregation of Gods is an extremely rare phenomenon, so much so that the Gods have no choice but to execute it in absolute secrecy.

(Can you imagine the riot that would erupt on earth were mankind to get wind of this clandestine rendezvous?)

The Gods all bring with them reams of paper filled with the unfulfilled wishes and prayers of their people; the Gods have all fallen behind schedule on fulfilling people's wishes and are hoping to gain some insights and new suggestions from their counterparts from all over the world on how to work their way through the lists swiftly and efficiently, all while managing well their stress and time in the process.

Some prayers they have been able to categorize and label

accurately, like the prayers of 10-year-olds looking for lost pets, or the prayers of parents seeking wisdom for their wayward sons.

Other prayers do not fall into any precise category, such as prayers for everlasting happiness or wishes for true love, for everyone has his or her own unique ideas about happiness and love.

Some Gods have longer lists than the others, and their paper bundles are heavier, and that explains their choice of mount.

Some choose to ride a horse, others prefer unicorns for speedier transportation.

Some others turn to wild cats especially if the wish-lists they carry are confidential and must not fall into the devil's hands at all costs, while some mount eagles or dragons to avoid the dangers that lurk on land.

The most powerful and swiftest of all Gods simply choose to fly in the night sky. They are a noisy, raucous bunch. High on nectar, they flirt with the moon and illuminate the sky with fireworks that dazzle more brightly than the stars.

If you look up at the right moment, you will bear witness to the goings-on in the sky but you will most likely mistake the boisterous Gods for shooting stars.

And you will make yet another wish, upon a shooting star.

But the flying Gods are too busy having fun to add your new wishes to their lists.

~

84

A SAFE PLACE TO HIDE YOUR SECRETS

The best place to hide a secret is to whisper it to the clouds.

Sing them a melody composed of your deepest, soul-scorching secrets.

Or pen a poem on paper, and set the words ablaze, so the wisps of smoke mingle upwards and disappear into the clouds.

Or blow all your secrets into a rainbow-coloured balloon and let it fly over the tree-tops into the blue sky and disappear into the white clouds yonder.

The clouds gather all your secrets by day, weaving together strand by misty strand of people's disguised truths.

And when night falls, they lay your secrets on the hillside, gently and quietly like a lullaby.

And then they wait.

Patiently.

Stealthily.

All night.

When morning comes, the clouds glide down the slopes

of the hill, biding their time, like a newly-wedded bride shyly lifting her veil to open up her heart's desires to you.

And where your secrets lay all night now glisten mysterious drops of dew.

Here now, gone the next moment.

And your secrets dissipate into the rays of the morning sun, leaving you to pursue the promise of a new day, of a new beginning.

85

THE PIANO MAN

Our town does not have a Pied Piper but we boast of the Piano Man instead.

No announcement precedes his arrival.

As summer rolls in and spills its warmth on rooftops and sidewalks, he makes an inconspicuous appearance in the verdant market square.

His piano, made of wood from trees that no longer grow on the face of the earth, rests under a leafy canopy like a fiery block of orange painted in the colour of sunlight.

His fingers, wizened and distorted by age and arthritis, skip and leap from note to note, white key to black and black to white.

Under his delicate touch, music spills out of the piano and mingles with the summer breeze and wanders into town.

It meanders down every alley and walkway, glides in and out of the busy market stalls, sneaks past the throngs of earnest shoppers and sly shoplifters and, when it chances upon keen listeners, sprinkles an extra dose of happiness on them.

His departures are as unassuming as his arrivals.

Quiet, unobtrusive, like the silent quotidian disappearance of the sun behind the twilight skies.

But every time he departs, he takes away a piece of our summer with him.

~

86

OF TALKING SCULPTURES AND TELLING FORTUNES

I wanted to know what the future held in store for me but my mother advised against it.

She was a skilled clairvoyant herself, so her refusal to read my fortune only made me more suspicious of the darkness I was sure lurked around the corner, preparing to engulf my path ahead.

I made discreet inquiries in town and learnt of the old sibyl who lives by herself in a red-brick cottage with red doors in a forgotten neck of the woods.

It took me six days and seven nights on foot to arrive at her door but when I did, the bust above the red doors said the old dame had given up the ghost last autumn.

Dejected, I plonked myself on the doorstep and mumbled a bitter *sorry*, feeling more sorry for myself than for anybody else.

But he told me not to be, for the wicked crone, *may her soul rest in peace!*, had never been any good at telling fortunes, he revealed.

I asked him if he could tell me my future instead but he

scoffed at the suggestion and said he did not hold with divination and fortune telling. Some things are simply not to be trifled with and destiny is one of them, he reasoned.

He offered to tell me a story instead, as a little reward for my journey, and, weary as I was, I took him up on his offer.

As I listened to his tale, for a brief while, I forgot to worry about my future.

~

87

I ASKED THE WISE OLD LADY WHERE I COULD FIND HAPPINESS, AND THIS WAS HER ANSWER

"There is a place on earth," she began, "where the blue of the ocean merges with the blue of the sky and it is no longer possible to tell where one ends and the other begins.

"Somewhere in that place lies happiness.

"You first see her from afar, like a sparkling jewel on the horizon.

"The road bends and twists and turns under your feet and yields occasional glimpses of the blue paradise.

"Another turn, and you think you will be close enough to reach out and grab her in your hands, happiness for you at last.

"You will not, of course, because it is the annoying habit of things living on the horizon that the more you travel towards them, the farther away from you they will appear.

"Eventually you content yourself with seeing her from a distance — isn't there already much joy in that? — and you tell yourself, surely, someday she will be yours."

I stared at the wise old lady in incredulity, my brows arched up like fireside tents. "Surely you do not expect me to believe that?"

She chuckled and gave me a toothless grin. "Any answer given is only as good as the question posed, m'dear."

88

THE GUARDIANS OF TIME

*I*n the beginning, there was only eternity.

Then Time was wrought into existence to give us a means to measure all that was finite and perishable, all that was mortal.

Harrumph! We all know how well that worked out, for truth be told, Time has been anything but precise.

Speeding up happiness, slowing down agony, snatching precious moments and tucking them into the hidden folds of the universe, the list of Time's mischiefs have quickly grown to be too long to recount.

Some said it was the past that was slowing down Time, his baggage of memories had become too great a burden to bear lightly, while others reckoned Time's journey into the future has always been one of haste.

The Gods were at their wits' end and pondered for days (or was it weeks or months? Time was too unreliable back then to tell!) until they agreed upon a suitable solution to tame the vicissitudes of Time.

All the memories of the past were to be entrusted to the Lion, all the dreams of the future to the Unicorn.

And as for Time himself, he was to remain in the present moment, bridging the past and the future, but belonging to neither.

I cannot fathom a punishment more cruel than a life devoid of memories and dreams, and so I tell Time how sorry I am for his ordeal.

But he simply smiles and insists that in being present, he too has become eternal.

～

89

THE FESTIVAL OF FOOLS

*C*ome, come, my friends, for today we celebrate our inner fools and imbeciles.

The reckless spirit that travels the world seeking the depths of her own heart.

The gullible lover who trusts you with his passions over and over again, for he has long lost count of the rusty nails you have driven through his soul.

The rebel, the renegade, foolish enough to risk her life for a future unknown.

The credulous soul who seeks out the innocence you have lost inside of you, for his world is a reflection of his own naïveté.

The daredevil, the foolhardy one, who throws caution to the wind and bares her subconscious to be trampled upon by the world in haste.

Oh, you fools!

When will you ever learn how wicked the ways of the world are?

Forgive us, m'dear, we are not wise, we know.

It is true the wise man knows only too well the perils of life and love.

But the fool simply lives and loves all the same.

90

COLOURS IN MUTINY

The colours are strewn about, remnants of a world that fell into ruin a very long time ago.

As if an angry child broke them into little pieces of chalk because they wouldn't stay within the boundaries she has outlined for them.

The elephants she had so painstakingly sketched in various shades of grey are now running amok, pinker than her rosy cheeks.

And the moon, the silver-coloured thief of light, takes to frequently disappearing from the paper, and when she deigns to reappear, is as blue as a robin's eggs.

And then there are the sheep, those innocent balls of wool, they keep morphing into black and now they don't look very innocent anymore.

Worse still are the meadows, where the grass grows greener and greener the closer they get to the horizon.

Her favourite was the Town of Shadows, silhouettes of minarets and skyscrapers, she had coloured them black as outer space, aglow from the light of the setting sun. And look, now her town is soaked in red.

And when they think she is not looking, all the colours fly across the paper like a flock of birds in a cloudless sky, leaving behind a rainbow in their wake, and spill over the edge of the paper like molten gold.

It will not be long before the child sees the wild beauty in their freedom.

91

A DOOR OF HEARTS

There are twenty-nine hearts in all.

Each has something written on it.

Most likely a blessing or a pithy saying, like you'd typically see on the slip of paper curled inside a fortune cookie.

Rarely, a command.

One, only one, has a curse written on it.

You can open the door to the other side only if a heart chooses you. And then its destiny becomes yours to carry, whether a blessing or the curse, or a vague aphorism that remains open to interpretation.

They are fickle, these hearts, and there is simply no way to tell whether they'd like you enough to let you through the door.

But if they do, don't think twice. Even if the curse is yours to bear, you are better off with a heart than without one.

92

INTO THE MAZE

Today, the maze is shaped like concentric triangles, with bridges strategically placed. Some to connect, some to divide.

You begin at the outside, and make your way in.

When you reach a dead end, as you surely will, simply retrace your steps to that familiar fork and go down the other path, the one you did not take the first time.

When you reach the centre of the maze, as you surely will, pause. If nothing happens, you can make your way out just as easily as you entered in the first place. Or you can choose to stay at the centre for as long as you can.

Occasionally, the maze will decide to burn all its bridges. Both the ones that connect, and the ones that divide.

Then you'll be left with no choice but to take huge leaps of faith.

93

STANDING STILL

*If I had to stay in one place for long enough, I might as
well be a tree, I suppose.*

How difficult would that be?

*To grow roots, commit my life to this patch of ground I stand
on, vowing to the soil that hugs me I wouldn't part from it until my
last breath.*

(Unless I were felled before I could die.)

But oh, young dreamer, don't you see how I billow with
envy come springtime, when the birds come from far-
flung places, their bellies filled with tales of all their
adventures,

and all I have to share with them are the same old stories
of how I stood still and tall,

watching other trees have their own exploits as their
leaves changed colour and deserted them,

how the snowflakes, gentle at first, settled upon us and

continued to pile even though our old branches creaked and groaned under their weight,

and how the snow slid to the ground and disappeared into it,

and how new leaves sprung up on the other trees and they all looked really cool, neon green and psychedelic for a brief while?

So tall am I that I can see all the way to the edge of the planet, the end of our world, all the places I'll never go.

I'd pout if I could, but I don't even have the means to complain to whoever made me, to rant and rave about how unfair it is.

Surely you don't want to be a tree like me when you could choose to be a flying bird or a scampering squirrel, a charging lion or an elegant giraffe, or a fiery star in the sky, if not a human being.

*Y*ou surprise me, you magnificent tree!

All I know is that the sight of you, standing steadfast and unwavering, evergreen and unchanging, reminds me that I too can hold my ground in a world that constantly compels me to be someone else, in some place else, doing something else.

94

MID-SPRING SNOW PARTY

No plans are made. No invitations are extended.

But at the first whiff of the possibility of snow in the air, long after winter has departed, the little ones creep out of their hiding places.

It doesn't take them long. This is one of those events they eagerly wait for every year — like New Year's Eve or birthdays — an unanticipated fall of snow in the midst of spring.

Everyone has a designated role; some bring out the cakes and the paper plates and the drinks and the glasses, some others bring out the harps and the fiddles, while yet others gather dry sticks and get a small fire crackling.

But the privilege of tying up the hammock goes to the oldest ones who know it's their last party.

And because they're so old and have learnt everything there is to know about life, they invite everybody else to join them on the hammock for one last night of celebration.

When the last song is sung and the last dance is danced,

the partygoers wake up the birds and the squirrels and beseech them to hop on the snow-laden branches of the trees and shower the ground with fresh snow so their tracks may be covered. Well, almost!

95

BELIEVABLE TALES

When my grandfather died, my mother told me he had to go away on an urgent mission.

I knew all about death and that everyone dies, sooner or later than we'd like, and that no one really knows what happens after.

But I also knew this was my mother's way of making sense of the loss of her father, and so I didn't interrupt her as she spun her yarn.

It was his job now, she said, to let the sun know every morning when it was safe to come out.

Grandpa surely knew a thing or two about safety. Judging by all the things he often said to me — don't go too close to the edge, the knife is too sharp, the fireplace is too hot — I knew he was the perfect person for the job.

I often looked for him at his usual spot, on the bench by the lakeside, but it was only this morning that I spotted him at the break of dawn, scanning the horizon and waiting for the sun to receive his message.

We had the most delightful conversation and once again

he gave me a crash-course on safety — never leave your drink unattended, keep away from lovers who take more than they can give, and always carry your pepper spray on you.

Later, when I told my mother about the encounter, she gave me a strange look and chided me for fibbing.

I couldn't understand why she wouldn't believe her own story, but she only said it was one thing to wish for something but quite another for it to actually come true.

96

HOPSCOTCH

*B*egin with the heart.
Always.
If it is light enough, leap on to the blue cloud.

Be warned, it has a tendency to drift.

If it pleases (I suppose tales of the land and the sea would keep the cloud pleased enough), it will take you to the peak of the tallest mountain in this world. And no, no human has ever heard of it, let alone set foot on it.

When you are ready to come down, step on to the narrow treetop bridge, which will lead you all the way down to the last ocean on the edge of the world. Its waters spill over the horizon, where a rainbow rises and disappears into outer space.

Only the blue whale can take you across the ocean. And no, no one knows when she will come, or if she will come at all.

If, for some really important reason, you cannot wait until the blue whale comes, don't lose heart, there is still the train journey to look forward to. I know how much you love trains.

No doubt you will surely fall asleep during the journey, exhausted from your adventures. But fret not, the train will wait patiently until every last passenger has rested well and is ready to depart.

There is only one station you can alight at, the No Exit station. There is nowhere to go from here.

But you can begin again.

Begin with the heart.

Always.

97

THE SONG OF THE RED BIRD

Red bird, red bird,
　　　sing me a song, you beg.
Sing me a song that will float on the breeze,
a song that will tickle my heart
and stir my soul, you say.

And the red bird sings,
a song only it can sing,
a song of remembrance,
a song of longing,
a song of all the places it had been,
of all the trees it had lived in,
of all the nests it had woven,
of the sole mate it had loved for several lifetimes
of the little red birds they had spawned,
of the squiggly worms and the juicy berries they had
fed their little ones,
of the way it used to spread its wings to teach them
how to fly,

how to fly away from their home, away from itself,
so they too may sing their songs,
to the ones who need to hear them the most.

And the song stirs your soul
and the tears spring forth,
and the red bird asks
if you have a song too,
a song you'd like to sing,
and you nod your head and say,
yes, I do.

And you sing about your life too,
and your story is just as old as the story of the birds,
and just as old as the story of the oceans,
and just as old as the story of the stars,
a grand story of so many beginnings
and so many endings,
tumbling into each other,
until you can no longer tell one apart from the other,
like the spokes of a wheel
disappearing into a giant disk,
the faster it spins,
until the wounds are no different than the joys,
and the scars and the smiles look alike.

When you sing the last note,
the red bird cocks its head to one side,
and says,
Why!
Your song is just like mine.

But how could that be, you wonder,
for the red bird is so beautiful,
but you,
when had you last thought yourself beautiful?

And the red bird flies to you
and brushes its wing across your heart,
and your spirits lift
and your melody floats on the breeze,
and you both sing songs that tickle hearts
and stir souls,
for the red bird has taught you how
you can only become the songs you sing.

98

UNINTENDED CONSEQUENCES OF DIETARY PREFERENCES

sst!

— Oh, hello there!?

Where are you off to?

— To the lake at the end of this path.

Come with me instead.

— Where?

(Points a paw towards the sky). Up

— No way can I climb that.

Won't you even try? I'll teach you.

— I don't have fancy ankles like you do, the kind that twist all the way and help you scamper up and down trees and walls and fences.

(Pouts a little, then sighs.)

— (Feeling sorry for the squirrel) We could play right here.

No. For the game I had in mind, we need to be way up there, on those high branches.

— (Knits brows and frowns with worry) What game did you have in mind?

The one in which we throw last year's nuts on all the people who walk down this path.

— What?! That's crazy.

(Shrugs) It's just a game. And no one will get hurt. And we'll have all the laughs.

— (Walking away, hurriedly) You're nuts.

(Shouts to the retreating figure) Of course. What's that thing you humans say?

— (Stops and turns around) What?

We are what we eat.

99

REQUISITE PARAPHERNALIA FOR YOUR JOURNEY

alling all travellers, wanderers, wayfarers, pilgrims! Please help yourself to these FREE offerings of items you'd find extremely useful on your journey, wherever you are headed.

Included are two leather suitcases — one large and the other medium-sized — both BRAND NEW, never used before.

The oversized orange shoes you see are a rare find. They'll shrink or grow to fit your feet. And occasionally, if they're in the mood, they can even make you fly.

The side-table is great for hosting roadside conversations at teatime. It is so pliable you can easily fold it into a square as small and as weightless as a handkerchief.

We've also added a few books you may find to your liking. And some light bulbs too, in case you spend the night in the middle of nowhere and need reading light. You can't always count on the stars; they're more fickle than you'd believe.

Did we mention all these are for FREE? They're yours for the taking.

There's only one condition though.

You must take with you everything on offer here, including whatever sneaked into those suitcases when we weren't looking.

HOW TO SOLVE A JIGSAW PUZZLE

First and foremost, count the pieces.

Make sure you have as many as you need, even if you do not have every single one.

Start somewhere, anywhere. It doesn't have to be an edge or a corner.

Start with anything that makes sense to you, anything that looks like it might lead to something bigger.

Do not be afraid to move on to another section if you've been stuck on one for far too long. Sometimes, you get a clearer view when you move away, a different perspective from another angle. And only you get to decide how long 'far too long' is.

And never forget this. A jigsaw is not only about the pieces that fit; it is just as much about the voids that need to be filled.

So allow yourself some artistic licence. The instructions never said you must use only the pieces you've been given.

Eager for more tales of whimsy and wonder? Dive into the adventures of A Benevolent Goddess, who is punished for her desire to help human beings but is unable to find salvation by any other means.

Alternatively, get this tale for free by signing up to my newsletter, Monthly Missives from The Dream Pedlar.
https://thedreampedlar.com/newsletter

ENJOYED TALES FOR DREAMERS — VOLUME I?

Thank you for reading *Tales For Dreamers — Volume I*!

If you loved the collection, I hope you will consider writing a short review—even a simple line or two—on the site where you bought the book.

Publishing is still driven by word of mouth, and when you leave a review it helps other readers decide this is a book worth reading. Thank you for your help in spreading the word.

You can also sign up to my monthly newsletter for updates on more Tales For Dreamers and other new releases, as well as heartfelt reflections on writing, reading, parenting and living the creative life.

Monthly Missives from The Dream Pedlar
https://thedreampedlar.com/newsletter

MORE BOOKS BY ANITHA KRISHNAN

https://thedreampedlar.com/books/

NOVELS & NOVELLAS

Dying Wishes

Finalist, 2023 Rakuten Kobo Emerging Writer Prize in Speculative Fiction

An expansive contemporary fantasy novel weaving Hindu mythology and South Indian folklore into a quest for belonging across different worlds — the World of Mortals and the World of Gods, India and Canada, the past and the present, the world outside and the one within.

Erased from Existence

An intriguing paranormal mystery in which a fifteen-year-old is erased from the memories and perception of everyone. Trapped in oblivion, she will have to unearth and reveal long-buried family secrets to escape.

The Land of No Reflection

A feisty fantasy tale of two sightless young women on the run from their homeland, having committed the unpardonable crime of seeing.

In Search of Leo

A heart-stirring fantasy tale exploring the gamut of emotions that loss and grief can stir.

~

SHORT STORIES

A Benevolent Goddess

An endearing story of a goddess who is punished for her desire to help human beings but is unable to find salvation by any other means.

The Mind Meddler

A thought-provoking short fantasy story on the games The Mind Meddler plays by sneaking thoughts into people's minds, until he meets the one person who can resist his unkind mischief.

Mrs. D'Souza's Dispute With God

A touching fantasy short story in which a school teacher, Mrs. D'Souza, dies unexpectedly and sets out in search of God to demand answers to her burning questions on life and death.

Your Mother's Nightmares

A bold collection of troubling, twisted tales scoured from the terrifying emotional depths of the motherhood experience.

~

POETRY

Hello, Dreamer! Poems & Dreams

An eclectic collection of 100 short poems encompassing musings on the universe and its mysteries, nature and human life, my secret longings and fears, love and heartbreak, the sun and the moon, the stars and the seas, light and shadow, and joy and nostalgia.

~

ABOUT THE AUTHOR

Anitha Krishnan is a speculative fiction author and an award-winning poet. Her fantasy novel, *Dying Wishes*, was a finalist for the 2023 Rakuten Kobo Emerging Writer Prize in the Speculative Fiction category.

She has lived in and left pieces of her heart in many places across the world including Singapore, Australia, Canada, and most of all in her beloved birthplace, India. She presently lives in Burlington, Ontario with her husband and their cherished child.

Find more books and her blog on the writing life at
https://thedreampedlar.com.

Sign up to her monthly newsletter at
https://thedreampedlar.com/newsletter
to receive heartfelt musings, exclusive updates, book recommendations, free fiction, and more!